Murder With Grace

A Play in Three Acts

by Leon Kaye

Based on the screenplay "Murder with Grace"

Baker's Plays
7611 Sunset Blvd.
Los Angeles, CA 90042
bakersplays.com

CAST OF CHARACTERS

GRACE NEVILLE - Grace, seventeen, cannot withstand impropriety or imperfection. While an idiotic comment may run off others like rain water, it gnaws at Grace, causing her much vexation. Smarter than anyone around her, she feels she can manipulate and outwit all to achieve her goals; peace and tranquility.

BETH HOBBS - Taller, prettier, and just as smart as Grace, Beth, nineteen, is Grace's accomplice and even mentor in deception. But Beth is more ruthless and seems to have no conscience.

HENRY HUNTINGTON - An enigma. Henry, twenty-five, tall and handsome, seems gallant and sociable. But it is a learned behavior, a mask Henry wears the few times he is in public. His emotions run deeper, and immaturity remains from his lack of interaction. Thus, he gets easily hurt, often walking out of the room or loudly proclaiming his opinion.

NAOMI TOURNEAU - Beautiful and thin, Naomi is as shallow as a rain puddle, and not as intelligent. Her interests are; money, jewelry, clothing, and home furnishings.

ELEANOR HUNTINGTON - Eleanor, fifteen is the typical gawky, plain-looking, approval-seeking teen. In Grace, she finds a sisterly figure and role model, seeks desperately for Grace's close companionship.

COLONEL HUNTINGTON - The Colonel, fifties, has seen everything and nothing could really shock him. Though he looks every bit his age, he relishes the company of young women, complimenting them at every turn.

JOHN NEVILLE - John, twenty-one, fair but expressionless, seems to have no emotions at all. He too is not exceptionally bright.

MR. NEVILLE - Although an attorney, Mr. Neville, late forties and amiable, does not seem overly educated. The home's patriarch, he seems very comfortable in his position.

MRS. NEVILLE - Mrs. Neville, forties, delights in John's future bride probably because she is even more dim-witted, if that is at all possible. She is either elated or wretched with despair. There is no middle ground.

CONSTABLE - A very precise, clear thinking man in his fifties. He dislikes the aristocracy, and worst of all – those who manipulate the system.

AUTHOR'S NOTE

I was writing a screenplay about a young woman that calls on the spirit of Jane Austen. The screenplay's title is *Plain as Jane*, and the young woman wants to become a romance novelist, yet her father is forcing her into taking over his insurance agency.

So I decided maybe it would be a good idea to actually read a Jane Austen novel first (watching movies doesn't count.) before delving into the script. I've seen all the major Austen films but I never heard of *Northanger Abbey*, so I decided to read that one.

While reading I came up with some wonderful ideas, and thought that Jane Austen was leading us down the path to a major embarrassment for her heroine. I found myself giggling just with the thought. All the signs were there. But Jane did not go that route. So I did, and the twist is what you'll find at the end of Act II.

At the time I only wrote screenplays, and tried talking myself out of writing a period comedy. I even wrote forty pages and tried stopping and left the manuscript in a bottom drawer, but the ideas and dialogue kept pouring out. I had wonderful lines and jokes, and double-entendres and a great ending in mind. So I finished the script and sent it out to production companies.

It placed in a few contests, and soon after, the producer of "Mrs. Dalloway" and "Richard III", called me from Alibi Films. She said she liked the script a lot and was sending it to London to be reviewed by the top brass there. Unfortunately, the deal fell through.

A few months later, I sent the script to Alpine Pictures in California. The reader and head of acquisitions both liked the script and were speaking with me about a sale. They needed the approval of their partners in Europe. But nobody wanted to fund a period film. Too costly.

So I turned the film into a play. I wrote it so quickly, leaving entire scenes in tact. I wrote the thing in a few months. It's since had a few readings but surprisingly, no one has produced it. Centerstage South Carolina offered a production but took back their offer two weeks later.

Maybe if this play does well, we can go back to Alibi Films or Masterpiece Theatre and give it another go.

ACT I

Scene 1

*(**SETTING:** The stage is split up into three rooms: Stage right is a dining room with a large table that seats six. Behind the table, upstage, is a door that leads to the kitchen, as well as a cupboard with glasses. Stage left is a door that leads to a second room, center stage. A couch is positioned in the room's center. Again, there is a door, upstage, that leads to the kitchen. The third room contains a bedroom writing desk, downstage. Behind, there is a bed with canopy. A painted portrait over the fireplace, at the room's back. All rooms are decorated using furnishings associated with the early nineteenth century.)*

*(**AT RISE:** The stage is empty. Only the happy, bellowing voice of **MR. NEVILLE** can be heard.)*

MR. NEVILLE. This is a day of great happiness, of the utmost…utmost…happiness. I scarce can withstand my great…

*(He glides, enters the room, a very happy **MRS. NEVILLE** a step behind him. Following is **NAOMI**, happy and wearing a frilly pink dress. On her arm is **JOHN**, amazingly expressionless. All enter.)*

MRS. NEVILLE. Pray, tell us of this great event. What has happened that has made you so…

MR. NEVILLE. Deliriously happy? Deliciously and deliriously happy? Devilishly happy?

MRS. NEVILLE. *(Her mouth opens as she understands.)* Oh…It cannot be…can it?

*(She looks to **NAOMI** for confirmation.)*

NAOMI. We are betrothed.

> *(With this, **MRS. NEVILLE** squeezes her hands together with great joy, lets out a high-pitched scream.)*

MRS. NEVILLE. Oh! My dear!

> *(to **MR. NEVILLE:**)*

You sly…keeping it so well!

> *(to **JOHN** while pinching his cheek)*

My little boy…Married!

> *(to **NAOMI:**)*

Oh!

> *(She throws her arms around the tiny **NAOMI**, hugs her a bit too roughly.)*

NAOMI. Thank you, Mother Neville. Thank you. Please!

> *(Meanwhile, **MR. NEVILLE** opens a bottle of champagne, begins pouring glasses. **JOHN** looks on with the interest of a stone.)*

MRS. NEVILLE. Well, tell me, my dear…

> *(She ushers **NAOMI** to the table, sits her down.)*

Was my John's proposal elegant? Or was he so overcome with love that he barely was able to intimate his meaning?

NAOMI. Well, actually, he…well he…

MR. NEVILLE. John did not actually propose to Naomi. It was handled a bit more…

NAOMI. Father did –

MR. NEVILLE. Yes, yes. I spoke to Mr. Tourneau on John's behalf. I merely told him how suited they were for each other – in age, physicality, station in life…

MRS. NEVILLE. A match made in heaven!

NAOMI. Yes! A match made in heaven! What fun!

> *(With this **NAOMI** lets out the most hideous laugh ever known to humanity. **JOHN** closes his eyes. Even the parents lose their smiles with this overwhelming surprise.)*

NAOMI. *(continued)* What would you have done, John, if my father did not say yes?

(Her laugh lives on.)

What if he said no, or even – maybe? Could you have lived? Could you have withstood another day without me?

*(The laugh is so bad, even **MRS. NEVILLE** watches Naomi in silence. **GRACE** rushes into the room from the hall, enters, eyes wide with horror.)*

GRACE. Miss Tourneau, are you all right?

*(**NAOMI** leaps to her feet, a sudden action which makes **GRACE** very afraid.)*

NAOMI. Grace, such news! We will soon be sisters!

*(Totally confused, **GRACE** looks to **MR. NEVILLE** for translation. But **MR. NEVILLE** is too much in shock to say anything. **MRS. NEVILLE** is also unable to move, standing with open mouth.)*

*(In an instant, **NAOMI** rushes to **GRACE** with open arms, hugs her. **GRACE** closes her eyes, withstanding the intrusion.)*

GRACE. Miss Tourneau, I am so happy for you. To who are you betrothed?

MRS. NEVILLE. To who? To John, of course.

GRACE. To John?

*(She turns to **JOHN** who picks up a glass of champagne, drains it in one gulp.)*

But how is it possible? John and Naomi just met…was it last week?

MR. NEVILLE. It is all arranged.

GRACE. Arranged?!

*(to **JOHN**:)*

John? Are you all right?

*(**JOHN** offers his glass to his father for refill.)*

GRACE. *(continued)* Perhaps, father...it would be better for all if...if we did not make this news known to...to...

MRS. NEVILLE. Why not, dear?

GRACE. In case...Naomi were to change her mind or –

NAOMI. Change my mind?!

GRACE. You have just met. And there are many things about John that most young women would find most unsuitable.

MRS. NEVILLE. Grace!

GRACE. Even charmingly so.

MR. NEVILLE. Grace, a word.

(He leads **GRACE** *through the door to the living room.)*

MR. NEVILLE. I do not understand you. Your brother will marry into one of the oldest and most honored families in all of England.

GRACE. Yes.

MR. NEVILLE. And it seems you are not happy for him.

GRACE. Yes. Well, no. I do not know what to think. It is true that her father is senior partner at Helmsley, Tourneau, and Hill. So the match is quite advantageous to you.

MR. NEVILLE. That is beside the point.

GRACE. And if John were to continue with his law studies, the match would make sense for him as well.

MR. NEVILLE. Yes. The match makes complete sense in all... in all senses.

GRACE. So it is decided?

MR. NEVILLE. Yes. John will continue his studies at the college while he and Naomi live here.

GRACE. Here? Naomi live here? But you heard her, father. You heard how she laughs.

MR. NEVILLE. I do admit it is a bit odd. But I am sure it is something to which we will all become accustomed. John did not enjoy squeezing mother's fistula at first, but in time –

GRACE. But father. That laugh – my nerves cannot withstand –

MR. NEVILLE. Come now, Grace.

GRACE. I am serious. I am quivering just with its memory.

MR. NEVILLE. In any case, you should be happy for John. You should revel in his happiness, as any good sister should.

GRACE. But is he truly happy, father?

MR. NEVILLE. Well…he did not say one word against my proposal.

(**MR. NEVILLE** *heads for the door. Just then* **NAOMI** *breaks out into a cackling laugh.* **GRACE** *closes her eyes, barely able to withstand its sound.*)

(**ALL** *leave the stage to the hallway.* **GRACE** *stands alone, centerstage.*)

GRACE. *(aside)* In the following weeks, I learned more than I cared about my future sister. The girl could prattle on for hours about some fashionable dress she saw while in Bath, or on endless gossip. Never a conversation about literature, or poetry – or even music. No location was safe from her intrusion.

(She walks through the door, stage right, to her bedroom.)

GRACE. *(aside)* The girl knew no privacy, no decency – and that laugh!

(From offstage **NAOMI** *piercing cackle resonates through the house.* **GRACE** *stands motionless, her entire body seems to convulse with spasms.)*

GRACE. The most odious, horrid sound known to humanity!

(**GRACE** *gets into bed.)*

Another day and I shall go mad. If not one day, then two days in certainty.

(**MRS. NEVILLE** *enters from upstage, a tray of tea in hand. She heads through the living room, into Grace's room.)*

MRS. NEVILLE. Come Grace, enough of this foolishness.

(no answer)

I know what will raise your spirits…

(GRACE *watches.* **MRS. NEVILLE** *lifts her skirt, begins to dance.)*

Tra-la…la-la-la-la-la-la.

(GRACE *rushes to her feet.)*

GRACE. No, mother. Please. The image will never fade from my memory and will impact me adversely.

MRS. NEVILLE. Oh? I am merely trying to raise your spirits.

GRACE. Thank you, mother. I am much better.

MRS. NEVILLE. Are you really?

GRACE. Yes. Thank you.

MRS. NEVILLE. All right.

(GRACE *heads back to her bed.)*

Let me see a smile.

(GRACE *stares at her mother).*

Come now. Smile.

(GRACE *forces a grin, then an ugly contorted smile. This pleases* **MRS. NEVILLE.** *)*

There now. Was that so unpleasant?

(MRS. NEVILLE *exits, heads back to the kitchen. Meanwhile,* **GRACE** *looks at her tea disinterestedly.)*

(Grace's best friend, **BETH HOBBS**, *immaculately attired, nineteen, enters stage left, heads through the house. She sticks her head in Grace's doorway.)*

BETH. Is someone here in need of pharmaceuticals?

(Instantaneously revived, **GRACE** *leaps to her feet.* **BETH** *steps into the room.)*

GRACE. Beth! Oh Beth!

(She hurries to **BETH**, *grabs her hands.)*

You have no idea what horrors I endure!

BETH. Indeed, I see. *(beat)* Your ma-ma' sent word that your nerves were in need of a tranquility potion, but it is worse than I imagined.

(**GRACE** *paces.*)

GRACE. Yes. Yes, my nerves. My nerves are extremely…very…

(She pauses, listen, motionless as a deer. **BETH** *eyes* **GRACE** *strangely.)*

GRACE. Do you hear?

BETH. Hear what?

GRACE. Laughing. Oh! It is in my head! Her laugh has invaded my skull!

*(***GRACE*** *grabs her head as if to squeeze out the intruder. She jumps onto her bed.)*

BETH. This is serious, Grace. *(pause)* Does this laughter belong to Miss Naomi Tourneau?

*(***GRACE*** *moans, lies flat on her bed.* **BETH** *neatly sits next to* **GRACE***.)*

GRACE. I am wasting away to nothing. Here, feel my arm.

*(***BETH*** *takes Grace's wrist, seems alarmed.)*

BETH. Have you tried ants in her bed?

GRACE. Yes.

BETH. Rotten eggs in her dresser?

GRACE. Of course.

BETH. Poison ivy in her stockings?

GRACE. I have tried everything. The girl is implacable. Like a cockroach she will survive us all.

(Thinking, **BETH** *stands, slowly heads for the teapot.)*

BETH. You know, Grace, if you are truly desperate, my father does have a vial of arsenic in his cupboard.

*(***GRACE*** *sits up.)*

GRACE. Arsenic? You cannot be serious.

BETH. Arsenic is supposedly instantaneous, and almost impossible to –

GRACE. No! No! To sit here and dream about it, revel in it,

that is one thing. But to actually –

BETH. You prefer to remain miserable?

GRACE. I cannot kill no matter how detestable…I mean, she is some form of human being. She must be.

(**BETH** *sits on Grace's bed.*)

BETH. Suit yourself. I was merely offering it up as a possibility.

(**GRACE** *sits next to* **BETH.**)

GRACE. No. We must put our heads together and find an answer.

BETH. Of course. *(beat)* We shall save the arsenic for your mother one day.

(**GRACE** *smiles.*)

GRACE. Beth, you always know what words warm my heart.

(**BETH** *drinks Grace's tea.*)

BETH. Now then, back to Miss Tourneau…What interests her?

GRACE. Yes! We must use her interests against her – but she has none. *(loathingly)* Except for jewels, and clothes, and all kinds of…

(**GRACE** *becomes suddenly silent.*)

BETH. What is it?

GRACE. *(carefully)* If there were a man…a man with a much greater income than my brother…

BETH. A rich man?

GRACE. Yes. If there were a rich man…and we persuaded him to pursue Naomi…

BETH. But why would he?

GRACE. Let me finish.

BETH. And she is already engaged.

(**GRACE** *stands, giddy with excitement.*)

GRACE. Yes. But what if we concocted his interest?

BETH. How?

GRACE. We can send the man adoring letters from Naomi, and craft romantic replies and –

BETH. No.

GRACE. – and then she will seek him out, and John will become insanely jealous, and their engagement quite precarious.

(**BETH** *shakes her head.*)

What?

BETH. The entire notion is ridiculous.

GRACE. Why?

BETH. No person would break off an engagement because of a few letters.

GRACE. We are not speaking about an ordinary person!

(**GRACE** *twirls in utter delight.*)

It can work. I know it can. I feel so much better. I am totally invigorated.

(**BETH** *stands, looks about herself.*)

BETH. Perhaps you feel well enough to clean this room.

(**BETH** *heads for the door, exits.*)

GRACE. Oh, yes. That is the easy part. The hard part is finding a suitable rich man for Naomi.

(*She sits at her desk, begins writing. A change in lighting reflects that days have passed.* **MRS. NEVILLE** *enters from the kitchen, goes into Grace's room, speaks – but no words come from her mouth.* **GRACE** *looks at her mother, smiles broadly.*)

GRACE. (*aside*) Such news! It is almost as if God himself willed it. He is so good and just! A rich man has come directly into our midst. Mama was at Crumwald Hall when Colonel Huntington and his daughter, Eleanor, first arrived.

(**MRS. NEVILLE** *exits to the dining room.* **GRACE** *seals her letter. She stands, fixes her hair while looking in a mirror.*)

GRACE. *(continued)* The Colonel's son, Henry, will be living there also. And Mama learned he was very much unattached!

(The **NEVILLES** *and* **NAOMI** *ENTER the dining room.* **GRACE** *hurries out to the kitchen with her letter.* **JOHN** *passes through to the living room.* **GRACE** *reenters. The letter is gone.)*

JOHN. Grace?

GRACE. Yes, John.

JOHN. You are worried about me.

GRACE. Yes. But all will soon be right again. You shall see. I have faith.

JOHN. Well…you need not worry. The incident with the ants –

GRACE. Yes, horrible.

JOHN. Yes.

GRACE. And so unusual – an entire colony of ants – to find their way into Naomi's bed –

JOHN. Yes. In any case, it seems Naomi is very fragile. I must take care of her.

GRACE. Do not worry, John. I will take care of her.

JOHN. No, Grace. She will soon become my wife. And she looks to me for comfort. It is a feeling I have never experienced – to be counted upon, to be the strength for another.

GRACE. You are my strength, John.

JOHN. Thank you. But this is something quite different. May I show you something?

(He pulls a piece of velvet material from his pocket, opens it, reveals a very expensive looking necklace.)

GRACE. A necklace? My goodness, John. That looks quite expensive.

JOHN. Yes. Naomi looked upon it at the jewelers and told me she expected it one day.

GRACE. Expected it?

JOHN. Yes. But not right away. She feels that with my future income, we should be able to afford many many fine pieces of jewelry. She will be quite surprised when she sees it.

GRACE. But John…that must have cost you…

JOHN. All I have, yes. But it is worth it to see her happy. When I save enough money, I will proceed to the second item, then the third. I believe if I buy one item each year, I can complete the list in my lifetime.

*(**GRACE** can only stare. **JOHN** puts the necklace back in his pocket. The others enter.)*

MRS. NEVILLE. Grace? Are you all right?

GRACE. What?

MR. NEVILLE. She is too thin. Grace, you need to eat more meat.

*(**GRACE** turns to **NAOMI**.)*

GRACE. Yes. I plan to.

MR. NEVILLE. Good. I do not want Colonel Huntington to think I have an infirmed daughter.

*(He sits on an arm chair, lights a pipe. **NAOMI** and **MRS. NEVILLE** sit on the couch.)*

MRS. NEVILLE. Have you invited Colonel Huntington to our home?

MR. NEVILLE. Not as of yet. But I am certain that in time –

GRACE. In time, yes. We need not invite him so soon.

NAOMI. Have you met him, father?

MR. NEVILLE. Met him? Yes. He is a fine man, and a good man.

MRS. NEVILLE. A rich man?

MR. NEVILLE. Yes, I suppose he is not left wanting. Yes.

*(**GRACE** gestures to **NAOMI** to come. **NAOMI** stands, heads toward **GRACE**.)*

GRACE. Perhaps you would like to take a walk around the room?

NAOMI. With you?

GRACE. Yes, of course. Surely you do not think I would want to see you walk alone?

*(***NAOMI*** smiles. ***JOHN*** sits next to ***MRS. NEVILLE*** on the couch, reads a book. The girls walk back and forth in front of the entire set.)*

NAOMI. I am sorry, Grace. It is just that some of the time I feel that you…I do not know how to say this.

GRACE. Sometimes speaking can be difficult.

NAOMI. Yes. For example, the night when the ants were in my bed…

GRACE. Yes?

NAOMI. You hit me numerous times.

GRACE. And I did apologize.

NAOMI. I understand. But still…did you think it necessary?

GRACE. Did you prefer the ant's horrible stings?

NAOMI. No. But you could have brushed them off. You did not need to hit me.

GRACE. You do have a point. I am sorry. In the future, I will bear that in mind.

NAOMI. Thank you.

(She smiles as if her previous thought has vanished with the wind.)

They say Colonel Huntington is very rich.

GRACE. Indeed. Mother did not let on. He is the fourth richest man in all of England.

NAOMI. But mother says he owns only a few properties in London.

GRACE. Yes. But such properties. Have you not heard of Windsor Castle?

NAOMI. Windsor Castle?! Of course I have heard of it! I have even seen it! It is enormous!

GRACE. And I have heard that the Colonel's son, Henry, is quite good looking.

NAOMI. Perhaps he would be a good match for you?

(NAOMI giggles, leans close into GRACE. GRACE forces a smile, a pained expression on her.)

GRACE. Yes. Perhaps, you are right. But everyone knows that whoever marries into the Huntington family, inherits the great Huntington jewels.

NAOMI. Jewels?

GRACE. Oh, yes. A vast array of rubies and sapphires and… and…

NAOMI. Sapphires?

GRACE. As big as your eyeball.

NAOMI. Really?

(NAOMI turns to the hall mirror, looks at her reflection. She raises a hand to her eye with forefinger and thumb extended, measures it.)

GRACE. And then I need not tell you of the opulence of Crumwald Hall.

(NAOMI turns with interest.)

NAOMI. Tell me.

GRACE. I have heard that the room cornices are painted with gold leaf. The front hall is of the finest Italian marble, and the gardens rival those of Versailles.

NAOMI. Versailles? In France?

GRACE. Yes, that one. I can understand your confusion.

NAOMI. It sounds like a palace.

GRACE. And the women that dine there must wear an entirely different dress every evening.

(NAOMI's mouth opens wide with delight.)

NAOMI. I have often thought that an excellent idea!

(MR. NEVILLE seems to awake from his thoughts, notices the girl's hushed conversation.)

MR. NEVILLE. What are you two prattling on about?

NAOMI. Oh, nothing of consequence, Father. Just idle

worship.

GRACE. *(whispering)* Idle gossip.

NAOMI. Idle gossip.

MR. NEVILLE. Come, Naomi. Why do you not sit with John? He is reading. Why do you not read with him?

NAOMI. Yes, of course, Father.

> *(She sits with* **JOHN**. **MRS. NEVILLE** *stands, heads for the dining room.* **GRACE** *follows.)*

GRACE. Mother?

MRS. NEVILLE. Yes, Child.

GRACE. Have you met Henry Huntington?

> *(***MRS. NEVILLE** *smiles, understanding exactly the mind of every young, unmarried girl.)*

MRS. NEVILLE. You wish to know if Henry Huntington is tall and handsome, do you not?

GRACE. *(with a blush)* Oh, Mother. You know me so well.

MRS. NEVILLE. Perhaps we will be planning your wedding in the not too distant future?

GRACE. Yes. Please, tell me everything about him. Everything.

MRS. NEVILLE. Well…Actually, I have yet to meet him. *(quietly)* But I understand from how the maid, Katey, spoke of him, that he is a very…economical young man.

GRACE. *(disappointed)* Economical?

MRS. NEVILLE. Yes. Do not worry, Grace. He will not spend his father's money foolishly on unnecessary baubles…

> *(seeing* **GRACE***'s disappointment)*

which is not to say he does not spend any money at all. I am certain he does purchase items that are necessary – much like yourself. You have always been very sensible with a shilling.

GRACE. Yes. Did Katey say anything about his appearance?

MRS. NEVILLE. No. All I know is that he resides in London. And he is very helpful to his father. He did not finish his schooling, but manages his father's properties and collects rents.

GRACE. A rent collector?

MRS. NEVILLE. Yes. A very sensible young man. *(quietly)* We will keep this young man away from Beth Hobbs. She is far too pretty a girl to be seen…I am not saying that you are not just as pretty as she.

GRACE. Thank you, Mother.

MRS. NEVILLE. You are both beautiful in your own way.

GRACE. Thank you.

(**MRS. NEVILLE** *exits upstage to the kitchen.* **GRACE** *turns to return to the living room.*)

BETH. *(offstage)* Grace.

(**GRACE** *turns to the hall door.*)

Grace, come with me outside. Henry sent a letter.

(*A glance to the living room, and* **GRACE** *sneaks out.*)

(*The curtain falls.*)

(*A moment later,* **GRACE** *and* **BETH** *cross the stage as if they are walking through the town. When they reach one side of the stage, they turn and walk slowly back.*)

(**BETH** *opens a letter, reads.*)

GRACE. When did it arrive?

BETH. I know the postmaster. He intercepts whatever I may ask of him.

GRACE. Does he really?

BETH. You have no idea how fortunate you are to be my friend.

(reading:)

Dear Miss Tourneau. I was very pleasantly surprised to find your letter welcoming me to the neighborhood. How very thoughtful of you to write.

GRACE. I have always found Naomi to be very thoughtful.

BETH. Yes, when she has a thought.

(reading:)

In answer to your questions, yes, I will be living with my father and my sister at Crumwald Hall. I do spend much time in London, but in that it is only half a day's journey, I shall come up every Friday, and leave early Monday. I am certain your entire family will be invited to a dinner party as soon as we are situated. I am quite eager to meet you.

GRACE. Oh, no. Beth, she cannot meet him.

BETH. Why not?

GRACE. He is a bill collector, and very frugal.

BETH. He is also very rich.

GRACE. I do not think so.

BETH. Not rich?

GRACE. From mother's description, he is no better off than either of our families.

BETH. So he is middle class. Well, if he is very handsome, then –

GRACE. No.

BETH. Not handsome?

GRACE. I am not sure. No one has seen him.

BETH. Are you certain you do not wish to use the poison?

(**GRACE** *gasps.* **BETH** *sighs. The task is more difficult than imagined.*)

I do not know what you desire me to do. I am not a miracle worker.

GRACE. Perhaps mother was mistaken. Perhaps the Huntingtons own…

(an idea)

It does not matter. As long as Naomi believes they are wealthy –

BETH. Yes. You must write Naomi a letter…a letter from Henry…

GRACE. Of course.

BETH. Let him state that he does not relate to others the particulars of his great wealth.

GRACE. Nor does he show it.

BETH. Right. And if someone characterizes him as wealthy, he vehemently denies being so.

GRACE. But he will lavish his bride with unimaginable riches.

BETH. And the keys to Westminster Abbey.

(The girls almost fall on each other with laughter, exit.)

(The curtain rises. Dressed more formally, **JOHN** *and* **NAOMI** *stand in the living room. The action spills out onto the downstage area.)*

JOHN. What is keeping mother?

NAOMI. She had cabbage for dinner.

*(***JOHN*** nods knowingly.* **MR. NEVILLE** *enters from the kitchen.)*

MR. NEVILLE. The Huntingtons will be here any minute. Where is your mother?

JOHN. Cabbage.

MR. NEVILLE. Good God! Has she lost control of her senses?!

(He rushes out through the dining room and into the hall, exits.)

NAOMI. John, I have not told you but Henry Huntington wrote to me last week.

JOHN. To you? Why to you?

NAOMI. I do not know. It seems the Huntingtons are very rich.

JOHN. Are they?

NAOMI. Yes. They own Westminster Abbey.

JOHN. Westminster Abbey? Impossible.

NAOMI. And they travel extensively. They have even been to Europe.

JOHN. We are in Europe. England is in Europe.

NAOMI. Yes. But I mean other parts of Europe – France, Belgium, India…

*(Dressed formally, **BETH** and **GRACE** enter from the hall. **GRACE** looks charming in her pretty gown. Dressed in a long velvet gown, **BETH** is stunning.)*

GRACE. Naomi, I would like you to meet my friend, Beth Hobbs.

(They shake hands.)

NAOMI. I am so pleased to finally meet you, Beth. I have heard so much about you.

BETH. And I am so honored to meet you, Miss Tourneau.

*(**NAOMI** seems pleasantly shocked.)*

NAOMI. To meet me?

BETH. Oh, yes. By Grace's descriptions, I understand you are quite an unusual young woman.

NAOMI. Unusual? Me?

*(**NAOMI** smiles, then cackles. It takes Beth every ounce of self-control not to step back.)*

JOHN. Miss Hobbs, I do not know if Grace told you, but Naomi and I were thinking of a spring wedding.

NAOMI. There is nothing in the world like a spring wedding.

BETH. *(whispering to **GRACE:**)* A spring funeral?

*(**GRACE** jabs **BETH**.)*

And I take it you shall live nearby?

JOHN. Actually, until I finish law school, our plan is to continue living at home.

NAOMI. It is only two more years.

BETH. Only two years?

*(She takes **NAOMI**'s arm, ushers her away, turns her head back toward **GRACE**.)*

Two years to some may seem an eternity.

*(An icy thought, **GRACE** seems pensive and nervous. **BETH** and **NAOMI** move away.)*

JOHN. I sensed some double entendre in Beth's words.

GRACE. Oh, you know Beth. She is always playing her mind games.

JOHN. If she disgraces Naomi, I shant speak to her again.

GRACE. Disgrace Naomi? No, John. Do you not see? She is secretly in love with you.

JOHN. With me? Well…that is quite different. She knows I am spoken for.

GRACE. The heart wants what it wants.

JOHN. Well, in this case, it cannot be.

(He heads out toward the hall. The doorbell rings. **BETH** *hurries over to* **GRACE.***)*

BETH. They are here.

*(***NAOMI*** *heads out to the kitchen, leaves* **BETH** *and* **GRACE** *in the living room. The two watch as the* **COLONEL** *and* **ELEANOR** *enter.* **MR. NEVILLE** *accompanies them.)*

COLONEL. Good evening.

MR. NEVILLE. May I take your coat?

COLONEL. Thank you, Mr. Neville. This is my daughter, Eleanor.

ELEANOR. *(curtsying)* Good evening, sir. What a pretty house.

(Through the door strides **HENRY HUNTINGTON,** *twenties, aristocratic, tall and handsome.)*

(Astounded, dismayed, **BETH** *and* **GRACE** *watch with mouths agape.* **HENRY** *pulls off his longcoat, reveals his strong, thin frame.)*

(The two girls seem lost in their stupor.)

BETH. …Grace?

GRACE. …Yes…that is my name, I think.

BETH. Tell me that is not Henry Huntington.

*(***GRACE*** *shakes her head, refusing to believe it.)*

GRACE. It cannot be.

HENRY. Good evening, sir. I am Henry Huntington.

(**BETH** *rights herself, turns to* **GRACE**.)

BETH. Do not worry, Grace. I shall straighten everything out.

(*She takes a step toward* **HENRY**. **GRACE** *grabs* **BETH**'s *arm.*)

GRACE. What do you mean?

BETH. I mean – your plan was a good one while it lasted, but –

GRACE. No, Beth.

(**GRACE** *frantically grabs* **BETH**'s *arm with both hands.* **BETH** *tries to pull away, cannot. She glares at* **GRACE**.)

BETH. Unhand me now.

GRACE. Please.

BETH. There is no way I shall allow that dimwitted cackling Naomi –

GRACE. Beth, you must!

(**BETH**'s *eyebrows rise with surprise.*)

BETH. I must?

GRACE. For me. For my sanity! Remember, all I did for you when you had that bad case of strep throat last year.

(**BETH**'s *anger cools.*)

How I fed you, and stayed with you, and even contracted the vile illness myself.

(*Softening,* **BETH** *sighs, watches as* **NAOMI** *and* **JOHN** *enter, meet the* **HUNTINGTONS**.)

And remember, Beth, he is a miser. And not rich at all.

(**BETH** *pulls her arm away.*)

Please, Beth. For my sake, play along. Remember, my nerves.

BETH. Yes! We must not forget your delicate nerves!

(*She enters the dining room,* **GRACE** *two steps behind her. As she nears,* **BETH** *develops a broad, plastic smile.*)

MR. NEVILLE. Ah, Beth, Grace. Come. I'd like you to meet Colonel Huntington.

(**GRACE** *watches intently, sees* **HENRY** *and* **NAOMI** *speaking, smiling cordially toward each other. The* **COLONEL**, *takes* **BETH**'s *hand. His leathery skin, from years in the sun, wrinkles in myriad localities. He gallantly bows.*)

COLONEL. Miss Hobbs.

(*Though plain-looking,* **ELEANOR**'s *eyes alight with the prospect of meeting new friends.* **GRACE** *smiles at* **ELEANOR.**)

BETH. Colonel Huntington.

MR. NEVILLE. His son, Henry.

(*Courteous to a fault,* **HENRY** *takes* **BETH**'s *hand.*)

HENRY. Miss Hobbs.

BETH. Mr. Huntington.

(*He immediately turns his attention back to* **NAOMI.** **BETH** *seethes.*)

MR. NEVILLE. And his daughter, Eleanor.

(*The girls shake hands, exchange hellos.*)

And this is my daughter, Grace.

(**GRACE** *approaches, a beaming smile on her.* **HENRY** *seems very interested.*)

HENRY. Grace Neville?

(**GRACE**'s *smile fades.*)

GRACE. I am sorry. Have we met?

HENRY. No. Miss Tourneau was just speaking of you.

(*Blanched,* **GRACE** *turns to* **NAOMI**, *who nods.*)

GRACE. Of…of me?

NAOMI. Mr. Huntington mistakenly believes I sent him a letter. I told him it was more probable that you sent it. After all –

GRACE. No.

NAOMI. You are very keen on sending letters.

GRACE. I did not.

NAOMI. And one of our servants delivered the –

GRACE. Please!

> *(Grace's outburst causes* **NAOMI** *to stop speaking.* **GRACE** *looks about herself self-consciously.)*

> I am sure the Huntingtons are not interested in our… obviously, neither of us sent the letter.

> *(***HENRY*** *notices* **GRACE***s embarrassment, smiles. The* **COLONEL** *chimes in, helpfully.)*

COLONEL. What does it matter? We have fine neighbors, some of them very beautiful – Miss Tourneau, would you care to escort an old man to the sitting room?

> *(***NAOMI***'s smile fades into an uncertain stare. She seems to look to* **JOHN** *for guidance.)*

NAOMI. I suppose it would be all right. You are as old as my father.

> *(The* **COLONEL***'s smile fades. He escorts her into the next room.)*

MR. NEVILLE. Excuse me.

> *(to* **JOHN***:)*

> Come, John. Help me with your mother. She needs much prodding.

> *(***JOHN*** *follows* **MR. NEVILLE** *out of the room.)*

JOHN. White rice works rather well.

MR. NEVILLE. We are beyond rice at this point.

> *(***ELEANOR*** *speaks a bit loudly to* **HENRY** *so that* **BETH** *and* **GRACE** *may hear.)*

ELEANOR. *(to* **HENRY***:)* How unexpected. You and father had such high hopes for Miss Tourneau, and now find she is engaged to Miss Neville's brother.

HENRY. Thank you, Eleanor. I was not more eager to meet Miss Tourneau than I was to meet Miss Hobbs or Miss

Neville.

ELEANOR. *(quietly to* GRACE:*)* That is not true.

(to HENRY:*)*

You even planned to escort her to church this Sunday. I know because –

BETH. *(to* ELEANOR:*)* Miss Huntington, there is someone I would like you to meet.

ELEANOR. Oh? Yes, of course.

(All smiles, ELEANOR *and* BETH *walk away, exit into the kitchen.)*

In the kitchen?

BETH. Yes. The dishwasher is a lovely woman.

*(*GRACE *and* HENRY *are left alone.)*

HENRY. Miss Hobbs is very kind.

GRACE. I have heard you are a…you live in London.

HENRY. Yes. But I sometimes find it a very distracting locale – with its myriad parties, restaurants, shops. One can have too many things to do. Do you not agree?

*(*GRACE *seems lost in his description.)*

GRACE. Indeed. How awful for you.

HENRY. I am glad father decided to move to the country. It gives me a chance to read, think, play the piano.

GRACE. Ah! You play the piano.

HENRY. Yes. Not very well, I assure you.

*(*GRACE *smiles blissfully.)*

Spending some time here also gives me the chance to meet new friends.

*(*GRACE*'s smile broadens, if that is at all possible.)*

Miss Tourneau was amazingly dear to write me a welcoming letter.

*(*GRACE*'s smile vanishes.)*

Your brother is very lucky to have her.

(**GRACE** *blankly nods. A moment later,* **HENRY** *turns toward the living room, then bows to* **GRACE**.)

I had better go in. Excuse me.

(*He smiles, then heads into the living room, sits with* **NAOMI** *and the* **COLONEL**. **GRACE** *stands in the door-way, watches.*)

COLONEL. Henry, why did you not inform me that you were in correspondence with this lovely young woman?

HENRY. I am sorry, father. It slipped my mind.

COLONEL. I apologize for my son, Miss Tourneau. Henry is a bit odd with people. He is much more at home with his horses.

GRACE. (*quite interested*) Horses?

COLONEL. Yes. Henry keeps six race horses.

(**GRACE** *swoons, holds onto the back of a chair for support. The* **MEN** *rush to her aid.*)

COLONEL. Are you all right, Miss Neville?

(**GRACE** *straightens herself.*)

GRACE. Yes, fine.

NAOMI. Grace so loves horses.

(**GRACE** *sees* **BETH** *and* **ELEANOR** *enter from the kitchen.*)

COLONEL. Miss Neville, can I get you some water?

GRACE. If you are thirsty. Excuse me.

(*She walks away from the puzzled* **COLONEL**. **GRACE** *takes hold of* **BETH**'s *arm, pulls her downstage and out of ear shot.*)

He raises horses, Beth.

BETH. What?

GRACE. He plays the piano, and he raises horses. I have never met a man that does either.

(**BETH** *stares hatefully at* **GRACE**.)

BETH. Oh, if I had the arsenic at this moment. We would

not be having this conversation.

GRACE. We cannot poison Naomi.

BETH. *(beat)* I was not speaking of Naomi.

(**BETH** *turns, sees* **ELEANOR** *and* **HENRY** *approach.*)

ELEANOR. Miss Neville, are you all right?

GRACE. Yes, thank you.

BETH. *(quietly)* Grace may be all right, Mr. Huntington. I wish I could say the same for Miss Tourneau.

HENRY. Is Miss Tourneau ill?

(**GRACE** *also turns to* **BETH**, *awaits some explanation.*)

BETH. No. I refer to the knowledge that her betrothed, John Neville, shall soon break off their engagement.

ELEANOR. But why is that?

BETH. I dare say that John Neville is a cad. Last year, he split suddenly with a very dear friend of mine.

(**HENRY** *and* **ELEANOR** *seem surprised.*)

My friend is only now getting over the pangs, but lo, I see the same in store for poor Naomi.

(**HENRY** *turns to* **NAOMI**, *who happily cackles loudly as she speaks to the* **COLONEL**.)

How she masks her despair.

ELEANOR. *(to* **GRACE:**) Why does your brother behave in such a deplorable manner? Does it not disgrace your entire family?

GRACE. Well…he…Beth?

BETH. I know him to be quite jittery. He often complains of his nerves.

(*She shoots* **GRACE** *a surreptitious glance.* **GRACE** *frowns.*)

Thus, he tires of one girl in a few months and grabs for another.

GRACE. Yes, that is true. He is the same way with food. If someone is eating a pastry, he waits until the person places it on their plate, then pounces on it.

HENRY. Good Lord.

(BETH *stares unbelieving at* GRACE, *shakes her head with distaste.*)

ELEANOR. And who is his next conquest?

BETH. Who?

ELEANOR. Yes, who does he have his eye on?

BETH. Yes, well…it's –

GRACE. Beth.

(HENRY *and* ELEANOR *incredulously turn toward* BETH.)

HENRY. Miss Hobbs?

GRACE. Yes.

BETH. No.

HENRY. But surely you would not fully entertain Mr. Neville's advances.

BETH. I…I am not sure…

GRACE. But John is relentless. He likens Beth to a delicate buttery croissant.

(JOHN *enters the room.*)

ELEANOR. There he is now. I scarce can look upon his face!

(JOHN *approaches* NAOMI, *sits with her.*)

GRACE. Excuse me.

(GRACE *hurries to* JOHN.)

John, if you need medicine for mother, Beth has come well prepared.

JOHN. Why did you not tell me sooner?

(BETH *walks across the stage, away from* ELEANOR *and* HENRY.)

Miss Hobbs? Miss Hobbs?

(*He hurries after* BETH. GRACE *smiles.*)

ELEANOR. He pursues her right in front of Miss Tourneau!

HENRY. The man knows no shame.

(The curtain falls.)

(Dressed in the same clothing, but with frocks and top-coats, the **COLONEL, ELEANOR, MR. & MRS. NEVILLE** *walk, bibles in hand, enter stage right, walk across.)*

MRS. NEVILLE. A fine service.

ELEANOR. But what can it mean, if your eye offends thee, to pluck it out?

COLONEL. It means, child, that one weakness will keep you from heaven's gates.

(They exit.)

(A distance behind, **JOHN** *and* **NAOMI** *enter* **GRACE** *and* **HENRY** *a few steps behind.)*

HENRY. I thought of Miss Tourneau most of the night. It must be a terrible life for her. I cannot imagine her pain.

(Eyes glued to **HENRY, GRACE** *blankly nods.)*

She is like a tragic muse, a beautiful, tragic muse, and a bold, strong, intriguing young woman. I could write sonnets for one such as Miss Tourneau. I could write a piano concerto.

(Spellbound, **GRACE** *stares at* **HENRY. NAOMI** *cackles ahead.* **GRACE** *doesn't seem to hear it.* **HENRY** *smiles.)*

You see. She laughs. How tragic. How tragic indeed.

*(**NAOMI** opens her Bible, a scrap of paper falls.* **JOHN** *picks it up.)*

JOHN. A letter?

NAOMI. A letter?

*(**JOHN** hands it to* **NAOMI.** *She takes it, quite curiously, opens it, reads. A few moments later,* **NAOMI**'s *face blanches. She lowers the letter.)*

JOHN. What is it?

NAOMI. Nothing. Nothing. It is a private matter…for us

girls.

JOHN. Who wrote it?

NAOMI. Who? Beth Hobbs.

JOHN. Again, this Beth Hobbs and her letters.

(**NAOMI** *folds the letter, places it back in her Bible.*)

NAOMI. Do not think about it, John. It is nothing.

(**JOHN** *nods, exits. Still reeling,* **NAOMI** *turns to look behind her, sees* **GRACE** *and* **HENRY** *approaching. Shaken, she exits.*)

HENRY. Look how she runs to him. The poor girl.

GRACE. *(lost in her thoughts)* Yes, the poor, unhappy girl.

(*All exit the stage.*)

(*A moment and* **NAOMI** *rushes onto the stage, enters, opens the letter, reads it.* **BETH**'*s amplified voice can be heard.*)

BETH. *(voice over)* *(overly dramatic)* My dearest Naomi, there are moments when a man must recognize the passion-ate fires that burn within.

(*A look of profound horror,* **NAOMI** *covers her mouth.*)

BETH. *(voice over)* I am consumed by your beauty, your smile, your delicate laugh…If it is not too late, I offer up my heart, as well as my extensive fortune. If you will have me, I shall lavish you with furs, emeralds, rubies, chocolates…

NAOMI. Chocolates?

BETH. *(voice over)* Fine linen, and the royal family jewels!

(**NAOMI** *sighs.*)

I also have royal blood and may one day become a duke.

NAOMI. A duke?!

BETH. *(voice over)* And wish you to be my duchess. It is a difficult thing to break off an engagement, but I am certain you have the temerity to do what needs to be done.

NAOMI. *(looks confused)* Temerity?

BETH. *(voice over)* I await your answer. At your service, now and forevermore, Henry.

> *(Faint, eyes fluttering, **NAOMI** puts a hand over her mouth, exits stage left.)*

> *(Carrying a bag of candy, **BETH** and **GRACE** enter right, walk across the stage.)*

BETH. I must admit, Grace. You were right. This is great fun – I do not know what to do next…

> *(Solemn, **GRACE** looks uneasily at her feet.)*

I wrote Naomi a letter and slipped it into her Bible at church.

GRACE. In her Bible?

BETH. An undying intimation of Henry's profound love. I wish I could have seen Naomi's face when she read it.

GRACE. You know, Beth, Henry Huntington is a very nice man, and I do not think it would be proper for us to –

BETH. What is this?

> *(**GRACE** sighs.)*

I knew you had no stomach for this.

GRACE. He loves fine horses. Don't you see?

> *(**BETH** seems confused.)*

He loves music, the piano, ballet, and poetry.

BETH. You are saying perhaps Henry is not a man?

GRACE. I am saying he is my…he is…

> *(**GRACE**'s voice trails off. She looks away. **BETH** stares sternly at **GRACE**.)*

BETH. How clever you are.

> *(**GRACE** looks up into **BETH**'s unflinching eyes.)*

You lure me into this game of yours to cast shame upon me –

GRACE. No.

BETH. So that you may have Henry for yourself!

GRACE. No! It is not true!

(GRACE *grabs* BETH's *hands.*)

Beth, I would never do such a thing! I am not devious. You know that.

BETH. Not by nature, but you have been in my company –

GRACE. It is just that I have found him so much what I have always dreamed of. I did not know men like Henry exist!

(BETH *stares angrily at* GRACE.)

But if you wish it…I shall relent. You are my best friend, Beth. I could never hurt you.

BETH. All right then. You say that you are not pursuing Henry, and I believe you. I shant pursue him either.

GRACE. Thank you, Beth.

BETH. But do not attempt to out-connive me. I do not take well to competition.

(*The two exit left. The curtain rises.*)

(*Seated in the dining room,* MRS. NEVILLE *wails.* GRACE *enters, then runs to her mother's side.*)

GRACE. Mama?

MRS. NEVILLE. Oh, Grace! Grace!

(GRACE *kneels before* MRS. NEVILLE.)

GRACE. What is wrong?

MRS. NEVILLE. It is finished! It is all a-a-a-rgh!

(MRS. NEVILLE *bursts into a loud, fitful blubber.*)

MRS. NEVILLE. No wedding! There shall be no wedding!!

GRACE. But why?

MRS. NEVILLE. I do not know! Naomi was just here! And she spoke with John and a-a-argh!

GRACE. It cannot be!

(GRACE *stands, hurries into the living room. Meanwhile,* MRS. NEVILLE *stands, trudges out into the kitchen, exits.* JOHN *enters to the living room from the kitchen. Morose, he stares into space.)*

GRACE. John? John, what happened?

JOHN. She broke off the engagement.

GRACE. Why?

JOHN. Does it matter?

(Suddenly vexed, **GRACE** *hurries to* **JOHN**, *grabs him by the collar.)*

GRACE. Yes, it matters! Did she not say anything? Did she mention anyone?

JOHN. Something about rubies and chocolates.

GRACE. Chocolates? What do you mean, chocolates?!

JOHN. Do you know her father immediately agreed with her decision? He never liked me. It seems I was not good enough for his precious daughter, me being a lowly –

*(***GRACE*** grabs John's arms, shakes them.)*

GRACE. Enough about you. Did Naomi mention Henry?!

JOHN. Henry Huntington? Does he have a hand in this?

(Holding back tears, **GRACE** *allows herself to fall back onto her buttocks.)*

GRACE. Oh John, how can everything go so badly?

JOHN. Fear not, Grace. I shall be all right.

GRACE. Oh, yes. Yes. You have cause for despondency as well. I am sorry that I am so self absorbed. It is just that I did not expect to fall in…

(Suddenly mindful, **GRACE** *catches herself.)*

JOHN. Fall in love? With whom?

GRACE. It is not important.

(She scrambles to her feet.)

I must pull myself together. Yes, that is what Beth would do.

JOHN. Beth Hobbs?

GRACE. Yes.

JOHN. *(stands)* You are in love with Beth Hobbs?

GRACE. No. Of course not. How can you suggest such a thing?!

JOHN. Well…I admit it is a bit odd, but –

GRACE. I must go. I must prevent Henry from making a terrible mistake.

(**GRACE** *heads toward the hall.* **JOHN** *follows.*)

JOHN. Henry Huntington?

(*A wail from* **MRS. NEVILLE** *echoes through the house, causes* **GRACE** *to shudder.*)

GRACE. Tell Mama I shant be home for dinner.

(*She quickly turns for the door.* **JOHN** *watches her exits, ponders.*)

JOHN. Henry Huntington and Beth Hobbs – I would not have guessed.

(*The curtain falls.*)

End of Act I

ACT II

Scene 1

*(**SETTING:** The three room set remains. The living room and dining room are switched so that the living room is stage left, perhaps with a fireplace. The dining room is center stage. The canopy on the bed [stage right] is removed. Other furnishings can be changed to denote we are in another home [Crumwald Hall.] The portrait also may be removed. Possibly, there is a window stage right.)*

*(**AT RISE:** The curtain does not rise. **GRACE** enters downstage, walks across the stage as she speaks.)*

GRACE. *(aside to audience)* This is not working well at all. Not well at all! I cannot allow Henry to go through with this, but what can I say to him? In jest, I wrote you a letter and signed Naomi's name? I encouraged her to break off an engagement to my own brother?

(She wrings her hands with worry.)

Kill her? No. I cannot kill another human being. God will most definitely send me to hell, and I have heard it is a most horrible place, much like the state of Texas in the summer.

(beat)

I simply must tell him the truth. I cannot allow a good man to make such a mistake.

(She exits stage left. The curtain rises, uncovers the stage described above.)

*(**COLONEL HUNTINGTON** and **ELEANOR** sit in the living room. A door pounds offstage. The **COLONEL** hurries offstage to answer.)*

GRACE. Oh, Colonel Huntington!

COLONEL. Miss Neville?

> (**GRACE** *enters in overly dramatic fashion. Concerned,* **ELEANOR** *stands, goes to* **GRACE***'s aid.*)

COLONEL. Miss Neville? What is wrong?

> (*The* **COLONEL** *takes* **GRACE***'s hands*)

GRACE. Everything. Pray, tell me, is Henry here?

COLONEL. Her hands are ice cold.

> (**ELEANOR** *takes* **GRACE***'s hands.*)

GRACE. I must warn your brother before he makes a dreadful mistake!

ELEANOR. Her hands are dreadfully cold.

> (**ELEANOR** *rubs* **GRACE***'s hands.*)

COLONEL. Indeed they are.

GRACE. 'Tis nothing, I assure you. Miss Tourneau has broken my brother's heart!

COLONEL. Please, Miss Neville, sit down.

> (**GRACE** *moves toward an arm chair in the room's center, does not sit.*)

GRACE. She has decided to break off the engagement, cause shame to my family –

COLONEL. By the fire.

ELEANOR. Yes, sit by the fire.

> (**GRACE** *hurries to a seat by the fire.*)

GRACE. Yes, yes, yes. I am sitting now. Will you be quiet?

> (**ELEANOR** *and the* **COLONEL** *seems surprised.* **GRACE** *too seems shocked at her irrational outburst.*)

I am sorry. It is just that I am so shaken. Is Henry here?

COLONEL. No. Henry is in London.

> (**ELEANOR** *sits next to* **GRACE***, retakes her hands. He pours* **GRACE** *a drink.*)

COLONEL. *(continued)* Is there something we can do?

ELEANOR. Her hands are like ice.

(**ELEANOR** *blows into* **GRACE** *'s hands.*)

GRACE. Well, yes. Indeed, there is. As I was saying, there is something most –

(**GRACE** *looks up at* **ELEANOR.**)

Most dreadfully, terribly –

(**ELEANOR** *raises the hands to her bosom.* **GRACE** *gently pulls her hands away.*)

My hands are much better, thank you.

(*to the* **COLONEL**)

Henry seems to be the center of a great misunderstanding. If I could see him as soon as he arrives, perhaps a great calamity can be avoided.

COLONEL. Miss Neville, brandy?

GRACE. Oh no. I do not drink.

ELEANOR. Nonsense. You are an icicle.

COLONEL. It will help, my dear.

GRACE. All right. Perhaps one drink.

(*She drains the glass in a second, hands it back to the* **COLONEL.**)

When does Henry arrive?

(*The* **COLONEL** *takes the glass, a bit surprised, heads back to the bottle to pour more.*)

COLONEL. Tomorrow morning. I am sorry, Miss Neville.

(*He hands her the liquor. She takes it, drinks it. She studies the glass.*)

GRACE. My, that is rather tasty.

(*She hands it back to the* **COLONEL.**)

ELEANOR. Do not drink too fast, Grace.

GRACE. Yes. The next two drinks I will drink more slowly.

(*She takes another, drinks half the cup, looks at it, then finishes it.*)

GRACE. *(continued)* A very challenging task.

(A bit giddy, she laughs. The **COLONEL** *too smiles with amusement.)*

ELEANOR. Miss Neville, Henry shall be here in the morning. Why do you not spend the night?

GRACE. Oh no.

COLONEL. Yes. It is late. And very cold.

GRACE. I could not impose.

COLONEL. It is no imposition.

*(***GRACE*** *hands the* **COLONEL** *her glass.* **ELEANOR** *stands, places a loving hand on* **GRACE***'s shoulder.)*

ELEANOR. Please, Miss Neville – stay. It is so awfully lonely here in the country. I do so wish to have a friend.

*(***GRACE*** *sips her brandy.)*

GRACE. Or maybe a sister?

*(***ELEANOR*** *smiles, turns to the* **COLONEL***, who smiles back at her.)*

ELEANOR. Oh yes – a sister.

GRACE. But not a nun. I would not care to become a nun – not even for Henry. As a nun, what kind of wife would I be?

*(***GRACE*** *smiles. Recognizing her lapse, she puts a hand up to her mouth. Amused,* **ELEANOR** *too smiles.* **GRACE** *downs another.)*

COLONEL. Perhaps Miss Neville would like to stay longer than one night?

GRACE. Oh, I could live here. But you would have to redecorate a bit. Perhaps an oriental rug in the foyer, a less gaudy chandelier…

COLONEL. I am sure that can all be arranged.

ELEANOR. Really, Grace? You would be my sister?

GRACE. Of course. But first, I must speak with Henry.

*(***GRACE*** *reaches for the brandy bottle.)*

COLONEL. I believe you have had enough brandy for one night.

GRACE. Oh no. I do not drink.

COLONEL. Eleanor, help Miss Neville to her room.

GRACE. There is no need. I can manage.

*(**GRACE** struggles to her feet.)*

ELEANOR. You are a bit tipsy, Miss Neville.

GRACE. Yes, I believe you are right. I do not feel well.

*(The **COLONEL** and **ELEANOR** help **GRACE** to the door.)*

*(**HENRY** enters, seems surprised to see **GRACE**, especially in her condition.)*

HENRY. Miss Neville?

*(**GRACE** seems shocked to see him.)*

GRACE. Henry?

COLONEL. She had a bit much to drink.

GRACE. Oh, no. I am not a drinker. It was…I was cold.

HENRY. Yes, of course.

GRACE. Can we speak? Privately?

COLONEL. Come, Eleanor. Will you be all right, Miss Neville?

GRACE. Of course.

COLONEL. We are letting go of you now.

*(They let go. **GRACE** swoons, grabs hold of the couch. They offer support.)*

GRACE. I am fine. I am fine.

*(**ELEANOR** and the **COLONEL** back away. **GRACE** takes a step, falls flat on her face. all rush to her. **HENRY** lifts her into his arms so they are face to face.)*

HENRY. Miss Neville, here, you must sit down.

GRACE. Oh, Henry.

HENRY. Come, to the couch.

COLONEL. You are not well.

ELEANOR. Should I fetch a doctor?

(HENRY *sits her on the couch.*)

GRACE. No. I am all right. As long as I am sitting. But I must speak with you, Henry. It is imperative.

COLONEL. We will be upstairs if you need us.

(*They exit.*)

HENRY. Can I get you anything?

GRACE. I have come…I have come to speak to you about Miss Tourneau.

HENRY. The poor creature, so horribly treated.

GRACE. No, Henry.

HENRY. No?

GRACE. John did not break off the engagement. She did.

HENRY. That makes little sense. Why would she?

GRACE. Why?

HENRY. Yes, why?! There is no reason! Because your accusation is false.

GRACE. No, Henry.

HENRY. Naomi is a sweet, brave and intriguing young woman!

GRACE. She is not. I led you to believe her mistreated, but she is not. I dare say that Naomi is a superficial, witless fortune hunter. That is why she broke off the engagement –

HENRY. Miss Neville, please.

GRACE. She fancies you only because you are more affluent.

HENRY. I can see why you are angry with her now, but there is no need to spread falsehoods –

GRACE. No, Henry. It is the truth. She did not compose those letters. I did! And the story about John and Beth – all a fabrication! There is no duplicity in John. He is home right now, anguished by her rejection.

(HENRY *ponders this as* GRACE *looks on hopefully.*)

HENRY. Whatever little prank you and Miss Hobbs have decided to play has no place in my decisions. I look into the individual's soul, and Miss Tourneau has a pure soul, unlike...well...I do not wish to continue with this conversation.

*(The wind gone from her sails, **GRACE** stares blankly down in her lap.)*

GRACE. I am merely trying to save you from making a terrible mistake.

*(**ELEANOR** enters, brings **HENRY** a letter.)*

ELEANOR. A courier brought this. He said it was urgent.

HENRY. *(reading)* From Mr. Tourneau.

*(**HENRY** opens the letter. **GRACE** looks surprised.)*

GRACE. But I did not send you...

*(She bites her lip, watches **HENRY** with the utmost interest.)*

Is something wrong?

HENRY. Excuse me. I must leave at once.

(stands)

GRACE. Is someone ill? Gravely ill?

*(**GRACE** stands, hurries after him.)*

HENRY. Miss Neville, this is a private matter. Excuse me.

*(He exits left, leaves **GRACE** wide-eyed with shock.)*

(The lights dim.)

*(Ten seconds later, the lights come on, find **GRACE** pacing in the bedroom, no longer affected by alcohol.)*

GRACE. If thy right eye offend thee, pluck it out!

(She mimes this action.)

And if thy right arm offend thee, cut it off! It is God's own will!

*(**BETH** enters from the living room, through the dining area, carries a bag as well as three dresses hung from

hangers, covered with a travelling bag. She knocks at the bedroom door.)

GRACE. *(continued)* Come in!

*(***BETH*** *comes in the bedroom.)*

BETH. *(scornfully)* Your mother sent clothing.

*(***GRACE*** *seems shocked to see* ***BETH.****)*

GRACE. Beth...I do not know what to say.

*(***BETH*** *lays the clothes on the bed.)*

BETH. Imagine my surprise when I came calling this morning, only to find out you are staying a week with the Huntingtons.

GRACE. It is not as you think.

BETH. You are not here to ingratiate yourself to Henry's family and cunningly claim him as your own?

GRACE. I came to tell him the truth.

(Angry, ***BETH*** *crosses to the window, stage right.)*

I wanted to stop Henry before he made a calamitous decision. Now he hates me and I cannot bear it.

*(***GRACE*** *quick-breathes with emotion.)*

Oh, Beth, nothing has progressed as planned. Nothing!

*(***GRACE*** *helplessly throws her hands up, sobs.* ***BETH*** *frowns.)*

BETH. Perhaps now is an opportune moment for a small present.

(A mischievous gleam in her eye, ***BETH*** *reaches into her pocket, pulls out a vial.)*

GRACE. Arsenic?

*(***BETH*** *smiles slyly.)*

BETH. One teaspoon of the powder, mixed in any liquid, will kill instantaneously. And you shall have Henry for yourself.

(**GRACE** *holds up the vial, studies it.*)

GRACE. Yes. If one were to commit murder, I believe arsenic would be the most proper method.

(**ELEANOR** *bursts into the room, enters.*)

ELEANOR. Grace?!

(*Fumbling with the vial,* **GRACE** *almost drops it.*)

Oh. I am sorry. I did not know you were here, Miss Hobbs.

BETH. What is it?

ELEANOR. Henry is back. Sadly, he has brought Miss Tourneau to spend the weekend here.

BETH. Ah, Grace. Opportunity presents herself!

(*Determined,* **GRACE** *nods, pockets the vial.*)

ELEANOR. Grace, would it cause you great displeasure dining in the same room as Miss Tourneau?

GRACE. Oh no. I do not mind. I would just love to have Miss Tourneau for dinner.

(*A pause as* **ELEANOR** *contemplates Grace's choice of words.*)

ELEANOR. You mean, to dinner.

GRACE. Yes. To dinner. What was I thinking?

(**GRACE, BETH,** *then* **ELEANOR** *enter the dining room, just as* **NAOMI, HENRY,** *and the* **COLONEL** *enter the living room from the left.*)

(*The former three girls walk through to the living room.*)

GRACE. Naomi, darling! So good of you to come!

(**GRACE** *outstretches her arms.* **NAOMI** *looks up with surprise, as does everyone.*)

NAOMI. Grace…I am so sorry about John. I do not know what to say.

GRACE. Nonsense. These things happen.

(**GRACE** *hugs* **NAOMI. BETH** *smiles, clasps her hands* *together.)*

BETH. It warms my heart so. They are like sisters!

(**ELEANOR** *raises a hand to her mouth.*)

COLONEL. I am happy there are no ill feelings.

NAOMI. Grace, I hope we can still be friends.

GRACE. Of course.

(She hugs **NAOMI** *again.)*

Till the end, my dear.

COLONEL. Why do we not have a spot of tea?

GRACE. Perfect, sir! You have read my mind!

(He heads toward the dining room. **NAOMI** *and* **GRACE** *follow.)*

BETH. Perhaps you would like to make us some of your cinnamon tea, Grace?

GRACE. Cinnamon…ah, yes! All of the most affluent people in Italy drink nothing else.

(**BETH** *and* **ELEANOR** *follow,* **HENRY** *trails.)*

NAOMI. I will try some.

ELEANOR. May I have a cup?

BETH. Yes. Grace and I shall prepare tea for everyone.

ELEANOR. May I help?

BETH. Yes, of course.

GRACE. Naomi, you sit down next to Henry, and I shall bring you the finest tea you will ever taste.

NAOMI. It sounds like heaven.

GRACE. Yes…perhaps heaven. Beth?

(**BETH** *follows* **GRACE** *upstage into the kitchen.* **ELEANOR** *follows. The* **MEN** *and* **NAOMI** *sit.)*

COLONEL. Did you ameliorate Mr. Tourneau's problem?

HENRY. Yes, father.

NAOMI. *(to* **HENRY***)* I must thank you, Mr. Huntington. It was very resourceful on your part.

HENRY. 'Tis nothing.

NAOMI. I do not know what my father would have done. Did the fire destroy all of his offices?

HENRY. Not all. But his men were able to move all of his files to the new offices. Sadly, some supplies and furniture were not salvageable. But things could have been a lot worse.

COLONEL. Henry keeps himself apprised of all real estate available.

NAOMI. Yes. Again, all of our thanks.

(Two teacups and saucers ready on a tray, **ELEANOR** *enters.)*

ELEANOR. Beth said these are for the men.

*(***BETH** *enters.)*

BETH. Here we are. Eleanor, this one is for you.

(She places it down on the table for **ELEANOR,** *next to* **NAOMI.***)*

And Naomi, darling, Grace will bring your tea in herself.

ELEANOR. *(shaken)* Grace will?

*(***BETH** *sits far from* **ELEANOR.***)*

I would like to wait for Grace. Miss Tourneau, you may have my tea if you wish.

BETH. No, no.

NAOMI. Thank you.

BETH. No.

NAOMI. I cannot have this cup?

BETH. Well…of course, you may. It is just that –

*(***GRACE** *enters, all smiles, with two tea cups.)*

ELEANOR. I do not have tea.

GRACE. What?

BETH. They switched cups.

GRACE. Oh. Perhaps if you switch them back…

(NAOMI sips her tea.)

NAOMI. Nonsense. This cup is perfectly adequate.

BETH. I will solve this. May I have tea?

(BETH stands, stares at GRACE. GRACE understands. BETH takes the tea, then drops the cup and tea all over the table.)

GRACE. Oh! Oh, what an accident!

BETH. How clumsy of me!

(The MEN stand, quickly raise the table cloth to avoid any spread of liquid. The women help with their handkerchiefs.)

COLONEL. It is all right.

BETH. A thousand pardons.

HENRY. It is all right, Miss Hobbs.

BETH. You may call me Beth.

ELEANOR. Fear not, Grace. I will clean this up.

(GRACE stares at BETH, motions to the bedroom. They both escape away.)

GRACE. That was terrible. I was so filled with wrath for Naomi, I did not consider the consequences of my actions. Everyone saw me bring her the tea.

BETH. If she died, you would have been hanged for sure.

GRACE. And you would have been my accomplice.

BETH. Accomplice? Well…let us not be so hasty.

GRACE. And what is this – you may call me, Beth?

BETH. I am merely trying to ward Henry off Naomi's scent.

GRACE. Are you certain you are not establishing a scent of your own?

BETH. May I suggest that we concentrate on the problem at hand – namely Naomi?

(ELEANOR heads for the bedroom, knocks, then enters.)

ELEANOR. Grace, Naomi and I decided to make a berry pie.

GRACE. Thank you, Eleanor. But I do not care much for

pie.

ELEANOR. We were going to trek into the woods to find some.

GRACE. Thank you, no. But have a good time.

(**ELEANOR** *nods, heads back to the dining room with the others.*)

BETH. You know, Grace, when one considers the many dangers that could exist in the untamed woods…

GRACE. Yes. Naomi may get mauled by a bear.

BETH. My thought was far more probable, and more hands-on.

GRACE. What is it?

BETH. It would take strength on your part.

GRACE. I am strong.

BETH. Strong enough to push Naomi from a high precipice?

GRACE. A cliff? Yes. I believe I can do it.

BETH. You are sure?

GRACE. Yes.

BETH. Let me see. Push me.

(*She turns her back to* **GRACE.**)

Go on. Do not be afraid.

(*as if scouring the landscape*)

My what a beautiful view. The people look like ants… wait, they are ants.

GRACE. Come now, Beth. Do not make me laugh.

BETH. Push me. Come now. Push.

(**GRACE** *pushes* **BETH** *hard with both hands.* **BETH** *barely moves.*)

What is that? I have felt winds more forceful.

GRACE. It was very hard.

BETH. Then take a few steps and do not be afraid to use your weight.

GRACE. I do not wish to hurt you.

BETH. You will not hurt me. Come now.

(**GRACE** *charges* **BETH**, *pushes her. This time,* **BETH** *falls forward, breaking her fall with her hands.*)

GRACE. Are you all right?

BETH. Good! You can do it, Grace.

GRACE. Yes, I can. Can't I?

BETH. You were a born murderess!

GRACE. Thank you, Beth. You always shower me with such compliments.

BETH. And deservedly so.

GRACE. I will do this, and show no remorse or pity.

BETH. Go. I will wait for you here.

GRACE. Thank you, Beth. It is best I go alone.

BETH. What about Eleanor?

GRACE. I can deal with Eleanor. I merely need to tell her to look for strawberries on the other side of the hill, and she will do whatever I ask. She is good that way.

(*In the dining room,* **NAOMI** *and* **ELEANOR** *have retrieved wicker baskets, head out the door, exit stage left.*)

BETH. Good luck, Grace.

(*She opens the door.* **GRACE** *heads out, rushes through the house and after the girls, exits.*)

(*The lights dim. A few seconds pass, and the lights return. The* **COLONEL** *and* **HENRY** *sit in the living room.* **BETH** *is gone.*)

(*Basket in hand,* **ELEANOR** *rushes into the living room, enters quite frantic and crying.*)

ELEANOR. Such horrors! Come quick!

(*She rushes back out. The* **MEN** *stand, quickly head for the door.* **ELEANOR** *helps a very dirty* **NAOMI** *in, enters.*)

NAOMI. My shoulder. It is badly bruised.

COLONEL. What happened?

ELEANOR. A terrible accident.

(**HENRY** *aids* **NAOMI** *to the couch. The* **COLONEL** *heads out the door, returns with* **GRACE**, *enters, hair disheveled and just as dirty.*)

COLONEL. Miss Neville…

HENRY. Eleanor, you explain.

ELEANOR. We were picking mushrooms, wild mushrooms. And strawberries. And there was even a tree with peaches, but they were –

COLONEL. The point!

ELEANOR. Yes, yes.

GRACE. It was an accident.

ELEANOR. A terrible accident.

HENRY. What?

(**NAOMI** *sits on the couch.*)

NAOMI. I was picking mushrooms by the side of a steep hill.

ELEANOR. I was on the other side of the hill, picking berries, and I heard a scream!

GRACE. That was me.

HENRY. What happened?

ELEANOR. Grace slipped.

NAOMI. All I remember is I jumped down a few feet from the ledge, and just as I did, I felt something very hard on my shoulder. Look, Henry.

COLONEL. Was it a rock?

GRACE. No, it was me.

HENRY. But how?

GRACE. I slipped.

ELEANOR. She slipped on the rocks. They were a bit wet.

NAOMI. My shoulder is throbbing.

ELEANOR. And Grace fell on her stomach, her body hanging out over the precipice.

HENRY. Good Lord.

COLONEL. Horrible!

HENRY. Should we summon a doctor?

GRACE. I am all right. No doctors, please.

NAOMI. Perhaps Dr. Hobbs can be summoned. I am sure he can give me something to numb the pain.

HENRY. Of course. Eleanor, go send a courier to Dr. Hobbs at once.

(**ELEANOR** *exits into the kitchen.*)

COLONEL. Miss Neville, you should be more careful in the future.

GRACE. Yes, I believe that to be a good idea.

NAOMI. Yes, Grace. You could have killed us both.

GRACE. I assure you that was not my intent.

(*She heads to the bedroom.* **ELEANOR** *enter from the kitchen, begins setting the table with dishes and glasses.*)

HENRY. Are you sure you do not wish to lie down, Miss Tourneau?

NAOMI. No. But I am terribly hungry.

COLONEL. Is dinner almost ready, Eleanor?

ELEANOR. Yes. Katey is preparing. I will help.

(*She heads for the kitchen, but the doorbell rings.* **ELEA-NOR** *reverses directions, exits stage left.*)

ELEANOR. *(offstage)* Beth, I am so happy you are here!

BETH. *(offstage)* Has something happened?

ELEANOR. *(offstage)* Yes. Something horrible.

BETH. *(offstage)* But what, pray tell could it –

(*They enter.* **BETH** *stops mid-sentence as soon as she sees* **NAOMI** *sitting on the couch.*)

COLONEL. Good evening, Miss Hobbs. Miss Tourneau is –

BETH. What?

HENRY. She has fallen.

NAOMI. My shoulder is badly bruised.

BETH. *(concerned)* Fallen? Where is Grace?

ELEANOR. Come.

> *(**ELEANOR** leads **BETH** to the bedroom. **GRACE** sits at the desk.)*

BETH. I take it…you are hurt also?

GRACE. Yes. All has not gone as planned.

ELEANOR. Grace, will you come to dinner in a few minutes?

GRACE. Yes. Thank you, Eleanor.

ELEANOR. You may dine with us too, Beth.

BETH. Thank you.

> *(**ELEANOR** bows, leaves. Meanwhile, the others head to the dining room, sit, as **ELEANOR** brings the silverware.)*

GRACE. How could I truly kill another human being? Is Henry really worth it?

BETH. I suppose no man is worth committing murder.

GRACE. If Henry truly wants to marry Naomi, then there is nothing I can do except be happy for them. And there will be other Henrys – other rich, handsome men that love all the things that I love – music, poetry, horses…

BETH. Come. Maybe a full stomach will help you overcome your heartache.

> *(**BETH** places a loving hand on **GRACE**'s shoulder, leads her to the dining room. All are sitting when **BETH** and **GRACE** walk in. The **MEN** stand.)*

COLONEL. Ah. Two very lovely women have arrived.

BETH. Thank you, sir.

NAOMI. Come, Beth. Sit by me.

> *(**BETH** sits next to **NAOMI**, **GRACE** on the other side, next to **ELEANOR**.)*

COLONEL. The chicken is excellent, Miss Neville.

GRACE. Thank you. I am not very hungry.

HENRY. Perhaps the mushrooms?

GRACE. No, thank you.

 (**BETH** *takes some food, begins eating.*)

COLONEL. You should eat something, Miss Neville. You need protein.

GRACE. Perhaps a little chicken.

 (*She takes the plate with the chicken, forks some onto her plate.*)

HENRY. It is understandable to not eat after such an ordeal.

ELEANOR. Yes, Grace. It has been a rather traumatic day for you.

 (**NAOMI** *quickly stands. Her face contorted, she clutches at the table cloth.* **HENRY** *and the* **COLONEL** *leap to her aid.*)

COLONEL. Miss Tourneau?

HENRY. Naomi?

 (**BETH** *and* **ELEANOR** *stand.* **NAOMI** *takes a step, clutches the* **COLONEL** *who keeps her from falling.* **ELEANOR** *rushes to Naomi's side.*)

 (*Confused, horrified,* **GRACE** *watches.*)

 (**NAOMI** *lies on the floor, writhes. The Huntingtons kneel by her.* **BETH.** *turns to* **GRACE,** *seems just as confused.*)

HENRY. Oh my God!

ELEANOR. What is wrong?!

COLONEL. Miss Tourneau?!

HENRY. Miss Tourneau?!

 (**NAOMI** *'s eyes freeze into a dead stare.*)

ELEANOR. She is dead.

 (**GRACE** *stands, approaches.*)

HENRY. She has no pulse.

ELEANOR. She is white.

 (*The* **COLONEL** *slaps* **NAOMI** *'s hand repeatedly.*)

COLONEL. Miss Tourneau?

(He feels her neck.)

HENRY. I don't understand!

COLONEL. She is dead.

ELEANOR. Oh my Lord.

*(**ELEANOR** turns, hugs **GRACE** who seems as confused as ever. Agitated, **HENRY** rushes from the room, EXITS.)*

HENRY. *(offstage)* Katey?! Mires?! My horse!

*(The **COLONEL** stands. Shoulders slumped, He stares at Naomi's lifeless body.)*

*(**GRACE** and **BETH** stare at **NAOMI**, then up to the **COLONEL**.)*

COLONEL. Come. Let us lift her onto the couch.

*(He approaches, but **BETH** and **GRACE** do not move.)*

Miss Neville?

GRACE. Yes.

COLONEL. I am sorry. You must not have ever touched the body of a deceased person.

GRACE. No.

*(She takes Naomi's feet. The **COLONEL** puts his hands under her arms, lifts her onto the couch.)*

*(**BETH** seems very shaken. She rushes to the bedroom.)*

GRACE. *(cont.)* Excuse me, sir.

*(**GRACE** heads into the bedroom, closes the door.)*

BETH. What did you do? Grace, I do not –

GRACE. I did nothing.

BETH. But how?

GRACE. I do not know!

BETH. *(begins to cry)* Is she really dead? Grace, I cannot bare it!

GRACE. But you gave me the arsenic!

BETH. No! That was not arsenic. That was sugar. Do you really believe I would have killed her?!

GRACE. What are you saying? You wanted me to push her from a precipice!

BETH. I do not understand. It did not seem real! But to see her writhe on the floor, to writhe in agony! I am sorry. I am sorry about ever speaking of murder.

(The **CONSTABLE** *and* **HENRY** *ENTER through the main door, speak quietly to the* **COLONEL.***)*

GRACE. Beth? You must snap out of this state. We had no hand in this murder. I know it, and you know it.

BETH. *(crying pitifully)* Did you kill her, Grace? You can tell me. I will not –

GRACE. No!

BETH. – tell a soul, you know –

GRACE. I said no!

BETH. I would never allow –

GRACE. Stop! I said no! I had nothing to do with this!

(A knock comes at the bedroom door. In walks the **CON-STABLE**. *Behind him, the* **COLONEL**, **HENRY** *and* **ELEANOR**.*)*

CONSTABLE. Miss Neville?

GRACE. Yes? Oh, Constable Jennings.

CONSTABLE. I am sorry to be blunt, but understand the circumstances.

GRACE. Of course.

CONSTABLE. Did you pick wild mushrooms?

*(***GRACE***'s eyes widen.)*

COLONEL. Eleanor told us.

ELEANOR. Naomi picked the mushrooms. Is not that correct, Grace?

CONSTABLE. Miss Huntington, please. We understand accidents can happen. But we still must know the particulars. Did Miss Tourneau pick all the mushrooms?

*(***GRACE*** turns, stares at ***ELEANOR***. Pale with fear, ***ELEA-NOR*** faintly nods. ***GRACE*** turns back to ***CONSTABLE***.)*

GRACE. *(carefully)* Yes, Naomi picked the mushrooms.

(**BETH** *turns to* **ELEANOR** *for confirmation.*)

CONSTABLE. All of them?

GRACE. Yes.

COLONEL. It was all a dreadful accident.

CONSTABLE. *(nods)* In any case, I shall have to make a report. There may be an inquest. Miss Neville? I did not mean to accuse you.

GRACE. I understand.

CONSTABLE. I shall write in my report that Miss Huntington and you were already questioned and free of any guilt. Miss Tourneau picked the mushrooms herself. I must go and break the news to her parents.

COLONEL. Thank you, sir.

ELEANOR. Thank you.

(**CONSTABLE** *nods to* **GRACE,** *leaves the room along with the* **COLONEL** *and* **HENRY. BETH** *squeezes* **GRACE***'s hand and follows.*)

Grace, that was quite frightening.

(**GRACE** *nods.*)

You are my dearest friend. I could never give you away.

(**GRACE** *pulls her hand away.*)

GRACE. Give me away?

ELEANOR. I did not tell them about –

GRACE. I did not pick mushrooms. Eleanor, you know that!

ELEANOR. Yes, I do. But you must admit, your eating no dinner could be construed as suspicious.

GRACE. I was not hungry.

ELEANOR. I believe you, Grace.

GRACE. You don't.

ELEANOR. I do. Believe me, I do. And in time, Henry will as well.

(**GRACE** *stares unbelieving at* **ELEANOR** *who exits. The* **CONSTABLE,** *the* **COLONEL** *and* **HENRY** *carry* **NAOMI***'s body offstage left, exit.*)

(**GRACE** *walks downstage toward the audience, glances periodically at the body as it is being carried.*)

GRACE. *(aside)* Though no one intimated the accusation, I felt that everyone suspected I had a rather large hand in Naomi's demise. Everyone knew that Naomi broke off the engagement one day before her death. Suspecting my guilt was natural. The problem was I too felt guilty. As the Bible says, in that I entertained the thought, I had already committed the crime in my heart.

(**BETH** *turns, stares at* **GRACE.**)

I am sure Beth suspected me as well. As did Eleanor, and Henry. But I knew those feelings of guilt were transitory and truly unfounded.

(*The curtain slowly falls.*)

(*The lights shine brightly on* **GRACE.**)

GRACE. *(cont.)* I did not kill Naomi. Her own stupidity killed her, which as horrible as it sounds, is very fitting. It is far better that she ate her own mushrooms, than if they were eaten by one innocent person.

(*The stage is empty.*)

I am at peace with myself. After weeks of reflection, the guilt is finally vanquished.

(**HENRY** *enters stage left, walks slowly toward* **GRACE.** *She sees him, freezes. They both stare silently at each other.*)

HENRY. Miss Neville.

GRACE. Mr. Huntington. It has been so long since we have seen each other. *(pause)* I hope Eleanor is well, as is your father.

HENRY. Yes. They are both eager to see you again.

GRACE. Are they?

HENRY. Of course. They consider you family.

GRACE. I did not think anyone wanted to see me again.

HENRY. Heavens! What gave you that idea?

GRACE. At the funeral, the way everyone looked at me. I could feel their –

(Overcome, she shakes her head. **HENRY** *kneels, takes her hand in his.)*

HENRY. Grace, no one believes you had anything to do with Naomi's death – least of all my father, Eleanor or me. We were there. We know what happened.

*(***GRACE*** nods.* **HENRY** *smiles, reaches to brush her hair out of her eyes. Before doing so, he thinks better of it.)*

Ah…well…I came to invite you and your family to a dinner party we are having for my father. It is his fiftieth birthday.

(He stands. **GRACE** *stares at* **HENRY** *as if in a trance.)*

Miss Neville?

GRACE. Yes.

HENRY. Will you come? I am certain it shall make my father very happy.

GRACE. Oh, yes. Yes, of course. I would not miss your father's birthday. He is a very sweet man.

HENRY. *(smiles)* You will grow to like him.

GRACE. *(aside)* I did not realize how much I loved Henry until that moment. How could I have ever given him up?

*(***HENRY*** walks away, exits.* **GRACE** *turns to the audience.)*

I surmised that it must have been part of God's immortal plan for Naomi to meet her end at the time that she did. It was like the tests of Abraham or Job. They had to prove themselves worthy of such a prize.

(The curtain rises. All are sitting in the dining room. **GRACE** *enters from the hall, stage left just as* **ELEANOR** *carries in a birthday cake.)*

ALL. Happy Birthday. Happy Birthday, Colonel.

(**ELEANOR** *heads over to the smiling* **COLONEL.**)

ALL. Good luck, sir. Many happy returns.

(*He blows out the cake's single candle. All clap.* **GRACE** *sits. When all is done,* **ELEANOR** *sits next to* **GRACE.** *Not well,* **MRS. NEVILLE** *leans over to* **JOHN.**)

MRS. NEVILLE. John, I am in some distress.

JOHN. Not now, mother.

MRS. NEVILLE. It was the beans, I am afraid. I am in need of a good prodding.

JOHN. But mother, I have not eaten my cake.

MRS. NEVILLE. Come along.

(**MRS. NEVILLE** *stands, walks,.* **JOHN** *sighs, stands, hangs his head as he follows. Both exit stage left.*)

GRACE. Eleanor, may I ask you, has Henry mentioned my name in the last few weeks?

ELEANOR. Oh yes. All the time.

GRACE. Really? Explain.

ELEANOR. He once said that you were quite intelligent.

(**GRACE** *nods half-heartedly.*)

And that you would be quite an asset in training his horses.

GRACE. Did he?

ELEANOR. Indeed.

(**GRACE** *nods, still not satisfied.*)

And that you had a charming disposition, and he liked you very much.

(**GRACE**'s *mouth drops open with profound joy.*)

He told father that just this evening. It seems they were discussing something quite significant.

(**GRACE**'s *eyes open wide. The* **COLONEL** *approaches.*)

COLONEL. Miss Neville, may I have a word with you in

private?

GRACE. Of course, Colonel Huntington! Of course, of course, of course.

*(Beaming, She rises. They head into the living room – alone. Meanwhile, **JOHN** and **MRS. NEVILLE** return, enter to the dining room.)*

GRACE. It is such a wonderful evening, is it not?

COLONEL. I admit I have something quite important to ask you? *(pause)* Miss Neville, we are all quite fond of you.

GRACE. And I with all of you.

COLONEL. One night, a month or so in the past, you stated that you would like to live in Crumwald Hall.

GRACE. It is a most beautiful house and I do feel at home here.

*(The **COLONEL** smiles.)*

COLONEL. What I am asking, Miss Neville, Grace, is – would you like to be part of our family?

GRACE. You mean marriage?

*(The **COLONEL** nods.)*

Yes! Oh yes.

*(Overwhelmed, she hugs the **COLONEL**. They both smile.)*

Oh! But where is Henry?

COLONEL. Henry? He is in the other room. Let us go and tell him the good news.

GRACE. Yes. Yes, of course. Actually, I do not know why he did not ask me himself.

*(The **COLONEL** laughs, escorts **GRACE** to the door. All are present.)*

COLONEL. Everyone? I have an announcement.

*(**GRACE** beams, stares at **HENRY**. He smiles warmly back at her.)*

Miss Neville has just consented to become my wife.

*(**GRACE** smiles broadly at **HENRY**. Everyone claps.*

*Suddenly, as if just hearing the **COLONEL**, **GRACE**'s ears perk. Her smile fades. She turns to him. She is immediately bombarded by a group of women, led by **ELEANOR**, who hug and congratulate her. The **COLONEL** takes a few steps away as men approach, shake his hand.)*

(The curtain falls.)

End of Act II

ACT III

Scene 1

(**SETTING:** *The two rooms, stage left are dark. Only the bedroom is lit.*)

(**AT RISE:** *Wearing her wedding dress,* **GRACE** *sits at the bedroom desk.*)

GRACE. *(aside, somberly)* Welcome to my wedding day. All young women long for their wedding day, and I... well, I wish Beth gave me the arsenic. That would be one way out. I cannot think of another. At first, I did not protest to the marriage because I felt some sort of heavenly justice was being served. This was God's own divine retribution. I was guilty and needed to be punished. But as time went on, I realized I could never consummate this marriage. To marry someone I did not love was a greater injustice than my botched attempt and thoughts of murder. Plus, Colonel Huntington was the oldest man I ever met.

(She looks around her room.)

I think to myself – you are a smart girl. Grace, you can find a way out of this. But I have tried. I have been thinking for days, and I cannot think of an escape.

(Dressed prettily, **BETH** *enters from stage right.)*

BETH. Grace? Are you ready?

GRACE. Beth, I do not know what to do.

BETH. That is a discussion you should be having with your mother.

*(***GRACE*** stands, paces.)*

GRACE. I do not want to marry him.

BETH. I cannot say that I am surprised. I surmised as much over a month ago. But Grace, the time has passed for second thoughts.

(**GRACE** *sits on the bed, head in hands.*)

Just think, Grace, he is a very rich man, and he cannot live much longer.

GRACE. How can I withdraw gracefully?

BETH. Withdraw? Now? Are you serious?

(**GRACE** *grabs* **BETH**'s *hand, stares into her eyes.*)

GRACE. Have you not heard a word I said?

BETH. Indeed I did. But withdrawal on your wedding day? Think of the disgrace, Grace. No decent family would have anything to do with you. No parties. People always talking behind your back. And no proposals – ever! Is that what you want?

GRACE. Of course not. That would be horrible. (*pause*) Pray, what would you do, Beth?

BETH. If you must, then go to him now and tell him honestly that you never loved him and this was all a mistake. Perhaps then he will withdraw.

GRACE. (*stares angrily at* **BETH**) That is the best you can come up with? The truth?

BETH. You have no alternative.

GRACE. No! There must be a way out of this. There must be a way I can not hurt the Colonel, and marry Henry.

BETH. Marry Henry? Now you are the joker.

(**GRACE** *stares blankly at* **BETH.**)

Come now, Grace. You did not think I would allow a man like Henry Huntington go to waste.

GRACE. You –

BETH. Yes. After you consented to marry the Colonel, I assumed the coast was clear.

(**GRACE** *seems unable to speak.*)

I wrote Henry telling him how badly Naomi's death affected me. Henry visited me twice and while in

London escorted me to the museum in hopes of raising my spirits. I am still quite shaken. Alas, Henry is the only soothing ointment for my wounded heart.

GRACE. I cannot believe you would…you…

BETH. I am sorry, Grace. But what would you do in my place? Come, let us be daughter *(pointing to herself)* and mother *(pointing to Grace)* and be friends?

GRACE. That is not funny.

BETH. You shall see. Years from now, we will look back at this moment and laugh.

(**BETH** *leaves, exits, passes* **ELEANOR** *who enters.*)

ELEANOR. Grace? Grace, are you ready?

GRACE. I cannot do it, Eleanor.

ELEANOR. Do what?

GRACE. When I consented to the marriage, I was under the impression your father was proposing on behalf of Henry.

ELEANOR. Henry? How could you think that?

GRACE. It was a mistake.

(**ELEANOR** *seems horrified as she understands everything.*)

ELEANOR. And the last two months? You could not have told my father? Before we made plans, you could not have –

(**GRACE** *stands.*)

GRACE. I do not want to quibble over details, Eleanor. I have made up my mind.

ELEANOR. Yes, indeed. You have.

(beat)

Would it change things to know that Henry will never marry?

(**GRACE** *stares blankly at* **ELEANOR**.)

GRACE. But he was in pursuit of Naomi?

ELEANOR. Not for himself – for father.

> (**GRACE** *is shocked.*)

You did not know?

> (**GRACE** *shakes her head.*)

Henry has never been really serious about any woman. Momentarily, he is drawn to the tragic, the downtrodden – the wayward kittens with no home, but in time, when the kitten is safe, he loses interest and rushes back to his horses.

> (**GRACE** *looks ill.*)

Henry can only fall in love with a woman so tragic, in so much perpetual agony almost unto death.

> (**ELEANOR** *holds* **GRACE***'s hand.*)

So you see, it is for the best that you go through with the marriage. It is the only way. The only way.

> (**GRACE** *pulls her hand away.*)

GRACE. I cannot.

> (**ELEANOR** *seems profoundly disturbed.*)

ELEANOR. But you do not understand. For us to be sisters, you must marry my father.

GRACE. What?

ELEANOR. You promised you would be my sister.

GRACE. Yes, yes. I thought one day I would marry Henry.

> (**ELEANOR** *turns sadly away.*)

Besides which, if I married your father, I would become your mother. So there you have it.

> (*Shaking her head, unable to accept* **GRACE***'s argument,* **ELEANOR** *sits on the bed.*)

ELEANOR. You promised you would be my sister.

GRACE. I am sorry.

ELEANOR. If you disgrace my poor father in this manner, he shant allow us to speak again.

*(**GRACE** sits next to **ELEANOR**.)*

GRACE. I do not know how I can tell him. He has been so good and kind.

ELEANOR. Do you not understand?!

*(**ELEANOR** weeps. **GRACE** eyes **ELEANOR** strangely.)*

GRACE. Eleanor, I do not know what to say. I cannot live the rest of my life with a man –

*(**ELEANOR** reaches for **GRACE**'s hand.)*

ELEANOR. You did not like Naomi, and now Naomi is gone.

GRACE. Eleanor, please listen to me.

*(**GRACE**'s eyes go suddenly cold. She stares into **ELEA-NOR**'s face.)*

(whispering) You killed her.

*(Sick, **GRACE** stands, staggers to the other side of the room.)*

You picked the mushrooms…and placed them in her plate.

ELEANOR. Naomi was a loathsome, odious person. If she were to marry father and move into our home, I knew you would never visit us again. It was you or her, Grace. I chose you.

*(**GRACE** stares blankly at **ELEANOR**.)*

Now, there is a choice to be made here. Either you come to the chapel and marry my father, or I go the Constable and tell him of your plot to murder Naomi.

GRACE. But I did not –

ELEANOR. You attempted to push her off the precipice. Do you think none of us supposed this?

GRACE. I see.

ELEANOR. So come. Marry my father and all will be well.

GRACE. I suppose I have no choice.

*(**ELEANOR** stands, reaches for **GRACE**'s hand. A moment and **GRACE** offers hers. The curtain falls.)*

*(The entire cast enters [except for **ELEANOR** and **GRACE**], wearing their Sunday best. The **CONSTABLE** stands ready to perform the ceremony)*

MRS. NEVILLE. *(to **BETH**:)* I am certain Grace will be very happy with the Huntingtons.

BETH. That was always her wish.

MRS. NEVILLE. And perhaps, Beth, one day you too will marry Henry. And then we will all be one family.

BETH. Yes, that would be a delight.

*(**ELEANOR** hurries in from the right, stands beside **HENRY**.)*

ELEANOR. She is here. Grace is here.

*(The **COLONEL** stands by the **CONSTABLE** far left as **MR. NEVILLE** takes his place far right.)*

*(Church music sounds. **GRACE** enters very calmly, takes her place by her father.)*

MR. NEVILLE. My dear, you are beautiful. Very much like your mother before child-bearing ruined her fine figure.

*(The organ blares the first bars of "The Wedding March." **GRACE** and **MR. NEVILLE** look up, but **GRACE** hurries ahead, arms up, waving as if flagging a car.)*

GRACE. Excuse me. Excuse me everyone. I have a confession to make.

*(Incensed, **MRS. NEVILLE** turns to **JOHN**.)*

MRS. NEVILLE. We are not Catholics. What is she doing?

*(The **COLONEL**'s mouth drops open in surprise. **GRACE** turns, stares at **HENRY**.)*

COLONEL. Grace, dear.

GRACE. I poisoned Miss Naomi Tourneau.

*(Many GASP in horror, MURMUR. **ELEANOR** is shocked beyond conception. Even **BETH** seems frozen with astonishment.)*

JOHN. *(to* **MRS. NEVILLE***)* I have always suspected her.

GRACE. I am sorry, Colonel Huntington. But I must do what is just.

(to the congregation)

I willfully picked poisonous mushrooms, and placed them on her plate.

(Gasps and murmers. **JOHN** *attends to* **MRS. NEVILLE.***)*

Constable Jennings, I implore you to do your duty.

(Confused, **CONSTABLE** *heads toward* **GRACE. ELEANOR** *leaps up.)*

ELEANOR. Grace, no!

*(***HENRY** *takes hold of the sobbing* **ELEANOR. MR. NEVILLE** *rushes to* **GRACE***'s side.)*

MR. NEVILLE. Grace, why are you doing this?

GRACE. The guilt is too much for me to bear.

COLONEL. But it was an accident!

MR. NEVILLE. I shall get the charges dropped. We shall plea temporary insanity.

GRACE. *(to* **CONSTABLE:***)* Is there need for manacles?

*(***CONSTABLE** *walks down the aisle at* **GRACE***'s side, leads her to the right side of the stage. There, a pre-built cage is lowered so that it encases* **GRACE.** *It may have four pillars of wood with netting stapled to give the imprisoned effect.)*

(All exit the stage except for **GRACE.***)*

GRACE. *(aside)* I had no choice. But I do have something up my sleeve. Let me tell you that.

*(***MR. NEVILLE** *storms in left and walks toward* **GRACE.***)*

MR. NEVILLE. The prosecuting attorney informed me that he allowed you to recant your entire confession. And you refused!

(no response)

I do not understand, Grace. There was no physical

evidence.

(again, no response)

They will try you as an adult. This is most serious, my dear. Please.

(again, silence)

Do you want to die?! Is that it?!

GRACE. Yes. I want to be hanged.

*(**MR. NEVILLE** stares blankly at her.)*

MR. NEVILLE. Why?!

GRACE. Because I deserve it!

*(Lost, **MR. NEVILLE** shakes his head.)*

MR. NEVILLE. You have gone mad.

GRACE. No, father. I know exactly what I am doing.

*(The **CONSTABLE** enters, stands next to her father.)*

CONSTABLE. Miss Neville, what do you say to the charges against you?

GRACE. I admit my guilt.

CONSTABLE. And do you also claim to be temporarily insane?

GRACE. No.

*(He turns to **MR. NEVILLE**.)*

CONSTABLE. The trial is set for tomorrow. There is nothing more I can do.

*(He walks away left. **MR. NEVILLE** follows.)*

MR. NEVILLE. She does not know what she is saying. She was always a temperamental child. This is just a tantrum.

*(They exit A moment later, **BETH** sneaks in from the left, enters.)*

BETH. All right, Grace, you have had your fun. It is time to stop this foolishness.

*(**GRACE** looks placidly toward **BETH**.)*

GRACE. I do not understand your meaning.

BETH. What are you trying to prove? If this is a ploy to get Henry back, then I relent. You may have him. Only please stop this now.

GRACE. If you wish to make such an overture, then do so. Only leave me out of it.

BETH. I will go right now. I will go to the Huntington's house right now and put an end to all this. Please, Grace, promise me then you will tell everyone this was all a mistake.

GRACE. I can make no such promise. But it is a very kind gesture on your part.

BETH. Then I will do it. If there is even a chance that you will tell the truth.

GRACE. You are a good friend, Beth. When I am dead and in heaven, I will look kindly down on you.

(**BETH** *looks terribly worried, hurriedly exits.*)

GRACE. *(aside)* I could never fool Beth so easily. I do not know what has happened to her sense of judgment.

(**HENRY** *walks slowly in from the left, enters.* **GRACE** *seems surprised.*)

HENRY. Hello, Grace.

GRACE. Henry?

HENRY. I gave the guard twenty pounds. We only have a few minutes together.

GRACE. How is your father?

HENRY. He is perfectly healthy, but shaken. He does not want me or Eleanor to mention your name ever again. *(beat)* I cannot stop thinking about you.

(**GRACE** *turns away.*)

I never realized what a bold, strong, intriguing young woman you are.

(*Her face hidden from* **HENRY**, **GRACE** *smiles.*)

GRACE. My trial is tomorrow. It shant take very long. I shall confess to the murder.

HENRY. It is so horribly sad.

(*His voice crackles with emotion. He paces.*)

GRACE. It will offer me great comfort if you attended.

HENRY. Of course, Grace, anything.

GRACE. And you may tell Eleanor she need not feel guilty. I shall take her place.

HENRY. Eleanor?

(**GRACE** *quickly raises her hand, covers her mouth.*)

GRACE. Oh. She did not tell you.

HENRY. Tell me what?

(**GRACE** *seems confused.*)

GRACE. I did not know. I thought she would have confided in you.

HENRY. Tell me what?

GRACE. I cannot say.

HENRY. Guilty of what?

GRACE. Henry, no.

HENRY. Did Eleanor know of the murder?

GRACE. No.

HENRY. Did she have a hand in the murder?

GRACE. There, you guessed it. I did not need to tell you.

(**HENRY**'s *eyes open wide with horror.*)

Tell Eleanor you guessed that she killed Naomi. I did not reveal it on my own.

(**HENRY** *stares blankly at* **GRACE,** *holds the bars of her cell.*)

HENRY. Eleanor?

GRACE. It is true, I had nothing to do with the murder. But Eleanor is my friend. I shall gladly go to my death to protect a friend.

HENRY. Oh no, Grace. You cannot.

GRACE. It is decided.

HENRY. I cannot allow you to continue with –

GRACE. It is too late.

HENRY. I shall go to Eleanor. She must confess.

GRACE. Henry, no. If she does, she will certainly be placed in a sanitarium.

HENRY. Better that than an innocent young woman be put to death.

GRACE. It is true. Eleanor is only fifteen. She will not be hanged.

HENRY. Yes. That is true. She must come forward.

GRACE. Your father will protest.

HENRY. I shall not tell him. Grace, my heart belongs to you. I am totally at your service.

*(***GRACE*** *stares at* **HENRY**, *nods. He exits stage left.* **GRACE** *smiles.)*

(The **CONSTABLE** *enters.)*

CONSTABLE. Miss Neville, the docket is full for tomorrow. We must have the trial today.

GRACE. Today? No, you cannot have it today.

CONSTABLE. There is not time for your tantrums.

(He goes into her cell, places handcuffs on her.)

GRACE. No. You do not understand. Henry will return with Eleanor tomorrow.

CONSTABLE. This is not a society party, miss.

GRACE. But my lawyer –

CONSTABLE. Your father is ready with your defense.

(He begins dragging her away.)

GRACE. My father?! No, I want a real lawyer!

CONSTABLE. You have already confessed your guilt. What more is there to say?

GRACE. Plenty! Please, sir. This treatment does not bode well with me. I shall report you to the head of the constables.

CONSTABLE. Yes, yes.

(He drags her offstage, exits.)

(MRS. NEVILLE, JOHN, *and* **BETH** *enters.)*

MRS. NEVILLE. I do not understand. She said she did not kill Naomi.

JOHN. But she did, mother.

MRS. NEVILLE. No.

BETH. She did not, John. I know this for a fact. And she said as much at her trial.

JOHN. Then why confess it so boldly in front of half of the town?

MRS. NEVILLE. To get attention.

BETH. No, John. She did it because I stole Henry from her. After I told him I wished no longer to continue our relationship, she recanted her confession. I fear I am to blame for all of this.

MRS. NEVILLE. But why did the judge not believe her?

BETH. Because she did originally confess to the murder. And there was sufficient motive. But that is not fair. Everyone wanted to kill Naomi. No offense, John.

JOHN. So she did not kill Naomi? Then I feel sorry for her.

(The **CONSTABLE** *leads* **GRACE** *back to her cell, enters.* **MR. NEVILLE** *follows, enters.)*

MR. NEVILLE. Fear not, Grace. At tomorrow's sentencing, I will plea for your life's imprisonment.

GRACE. Will somebody please help me?!

CONSTABLE. Quiet, miss. To think, I was gentle to you when this incident first occurred. Mr. and Mrs. Tourneau requested a full investigation, but I refused. Because I believed you. And now, what a fool I must look to you, and to everyone in this corner of the world. I will not be fooled again.

(He turns, storms away, exits stage left.)

GRACE. I have apologized to him more than once. I do not understand his attitude.

*(***HENRY*** enters.* **GRACE** *beams when she sees him.)*

GRACE. *(continued)* Oh, Henry!

HENRY. I am sorry, Grace.

GRACE. Where is Eleanor?

HENRY. She would not come.

GRACE. What do you mean? She must come. She must come forward before six o'clock. Otherwise –

HENRY. I have tried to convince her. She is implacable!

GRACE. You must try again! Go now! Let her come now, as soon as she can! Please, Henry!

*(**HENRY** bows, rushes off, exits.)*

JOHN. Grace, what has Eleanor Huntington have to do with this?

GRACE. She…she can state for a fact that I did not kill Naomi.

MR. NEVILLE. How so? For a fact?

MRS. NEVILLE. How can she do that?

GRACE. Because she can.

BETH. *(understanding)* Because…because she killed Naomi.

(All are quiet with understanding.)

MR. NEVILLE. And you wanted to take the blame for a friend? How idiotic!

MRS. NEVILLE. Yes, Grace. I did not raise you to commit such noble actions!

GRACE. I need you all to go to Colonel Huntington and plead my case to him. I know I have hurt him –

JOHN. Emasculated him.

GRACE. Yes, whatever – but am I truly worthy of death? I understand he is angry, but does he want me to die?

(All ponder this.)

MRS. NEVILLE. Can we give him a few days to cool off?

GRACE. No, mother. I will be hanged in fourteen hours! You must act quickly!

JOHN. Yes. Come, father. Let us run.

MR. NEVILLE. Yes. You run. I shall walk rather quickly.

(They exit.)

BETH. I will speak to the Colonel myself. Perhaps a warm smile and soft hand will soothe the savage breast.

GRACE. Yes, thank you, Beth. And wear something more becoming than what you are wearing. Please. It is too important.

BETH. I shall wear the black satin.

GRACE. Good. Perfect.

(She hurries off, exits.)

MRS. NEVILLE. And should I go and plead with the judge to remit your sentence?

GRACE. What have you eaten today?

MRS. NEVILLE. Pork.

GRACE. Perhaps it would be better if you went home. Rest and be here at four.

MRS. NEVILLE. Four in the morning?

GRACE. Yes, Mother. I would see you at a better hour, but I am not in control of such matters.

*(**MRS. NEVILLE** holds **GRACE**'s hand through the bars.)*

MRS. NEVILLE. Oh, my pretty, pretty girl. *(beat)* Such a thin pretty neck –

(raising a handkerchief to her eyes)

It will snap like a twig.

(She exits. The lights dim.)

*(A minute and the lights rise yet it is not bright – symbolifying very early morning. The **CONSTABLE** enters.)*

CONSTABLE. Are you ready, Miss Neville?

GRACE. Ready? What time is it?

CONSTABLE. It is not yet five.

GRACE. But…but I am to be hanged at six.

CONSTABLE. Are you not eager to meet your maker?

GRACE. My family is on its way. They wish to say their good-byes!

(He enters her cell.)

CONSTABLE. I am sure Miss Tourneau would have liked to say goodbye to her family as well.

GRACE. Yes, good point. But…AH! Here they are!

(The **NEVILLES** *arrive, enter.)*

MR. NEVILLE. What is this?

GRACE. Father, help me.

MR. NEVILLE. Sir, the orders were not until six a.m. You must give us time to say goodbye.

CONSTABLE. You have five minutes.

> *(***MR. NEVILLE** *stares at the* **CONSTABLE** *who stares evilly back.* **MR. NEVILLE** *seems shaken.)*

MR. NEVILLE. We, sir, will take our time.

> *(quietly to* **MRS. NEVILLE***)*

We must make this quick. The man has the eyes of the devil himself.

> *(***MRS. NEVILLE** *and* **GRACE** *embrace.)*

GRACE. Goodbye, Mother.

MRS. NEVILLE. What shall I do without you?

> *(She puts a hand to* **GRACE***'s cheek, then pushes the hair from* **GRACE***'s forehead, fixes it.)*

GRACE. John?

> *(They hug.)*

JOHN. I want you to know that although I will leave before the hanging, my prayers are with you, Grace. These hangings are a grisly business and I must think of my sanity after witnessing such a horrible…

> *(He sees* **GRACE***'s feared expression.)*

Yes, well…. good luck.

> *(She hugs* **MR. NEVILLE.***)*

GRACE. I am sorry, Father. You may not think ill of me, and though I am innocent of Naomi's murder…I do deserve to be punished.

MR. NEVILLE. All of us do, child. All of us do.

CONSTABLE. All right, Miss Neville.

(She takes a deep breath, summons courage.)

GRACE. I am ready.

(A noose falls from the rafters, stage left.)

Ah-h-h! No! I am too young!

(The **CONSTABLE** *drags her to the noose.)*

It is not fair! This is not justice! No!

(The **CONSTABLE** *places the noose around her neck.)*

Father?! Help me!

(Suddenly, **HENRY** *enters from the right. The* **COLONEL,** **BETH** *and* **ELEANOR** *follow.)*

HENRY. Stop! Stop!

*(***GRACE** *smiles.)*

GRACE. HENRY?! And ELEANOR!!

HENRY. Grace?! I've brought Eleanor!

GRACE. ELEANOR?!

(The Nevilles rush toward the **COLONEL** *and* **ELEA-NOR,** *lead them toward* **GRACE.***)*

HENRY. Grace?! She will admit her guilt!

ELEANOR. Grace, I am sorry.

GRACE. It is all right.

COLONEL. I was angry, but I did not realize –

ELEANOR. I was afraid, Grace.

GRACE. Eleanor, you must confess now!

ELEANOR. Yes. I confess. I am the one that poisoned Naomi – not Grace. I confess!

(The **CONSTABLE** *holds his hand out, quiets the crowd.)*

GRACE. There, you see. She confessed!

CONSTABLE. I am not a judge.

GRACE. What? What do you mean?

CONSTABLE. I mean – you have been found guilty in a court of law. You will hang this morning, miss.

(The **CONSTABLE** *tightens the noose around* **GRACE**'s *neck. She opens her mouth, tries to scream.)*

HENRY. Stop!

(All turn to him.)

(motioning to the audience)

There is a great crowd of people here – a great number of people who know what has happened. Let their judgment be sacrosanct. They are a jury unlike any other. They have witnessed all of these events! They know that Miss Neville is innocent. Do you not?!

(pause for the audience's reaction)

*(***HENRY** *seems very satisfied.)*

CONSTABLE. And just as many find her a spoiled, prissy, manipulator. She has lied to her parents, her brother, her best friend, and has made merry at their expense. She even used the criminal court system – and to what end? To win the affection of an immature, possibly homosexual, flake! She is deserving of some punishment. I cannot merely release her! That is not justice!

(The cast objects.)

ELEANOR. What if…what if she were to do service to the poor?

CONSTABLE. She should already be doing as much.

(Grace's family looks away, as does **GRACE**.*)*

You have done nothing for the poor, have you?

GRACE. Truthfully, I did plan on in. Beth, did I not say as much last week – how I planned on throwing a ball for the less fortunate?

BETH. Yes, that is true. She did –

CONSTABLE. Quiet! As if the poor need wine and song to remind them of their miseries!

JOHN. *(to* **MR. NEVILLE***)* What if she made nice to him?

MR. NEVILLE. What?

JOHN. A little nice-nice is a small price to pay –

MR. NEVILLE. Certainly not!

MRS. NEVILLE. Please, sir. I beg of you, allow my Grace to go free.

CONSTABLE. And what is your argument?

MRS. NEVILLE. Argument? It is just that…the rope is chafing her pretty neck.

CONSTABLE. Well, we can put an end to that, can we not?

GRACE. NO!

> (**ALL** *turn to* **GRACE.***)*

> Sir, you are concerned that I have not learned anything. You believe that I may deceive and misuse the trust of others. I assure you I shall never do these things again. I understand I have mistreated my family, the Huntingtons, even Beth –

CONSTABLE. And me.

GRACE. And you of course. Of course, you. Please, sir, have mercy upon me.

> (**CONSTABLE** *stares at* **GRACE,** *then turns away.)*

CONSTABLE. That is not enough. She must be punished.

HENRY. Punished?! Oh, enough of this charade of a trial!

CONSTABLE. Charade?

HENRY. Yes. This is not justice. You are but one man, one frustrated old man.

> (*Cast members try to quiet* **HENRY.***)*

> You clamor for justice. You would not even know what it is if it bit you on the bottom.

COLONEL. Enough, Henry.

HENRY. No, father. I have learned to stand up to bullies such as he. Listen to the pleas of friends, relatives, and this good crowd. They are good people, and their ruling should be esteemed. Hear them when they chant, "Let Grace go. Let Grace go."

(Uncertain, the cast joins in. As the crowd chants, the **CONSTABLE** *seethes in anger.)*

CONSTABLE. QUIET! I have never seen such indulgent and dissolute people! It seems I am the only one with any concept of justice in this room! And I alone must make the decision.

(to the crowd)

Take heart to know your pleas for mercy have not saved Miss Neville. They have finished her!

(With this he pulls a rope or lever. The theater goes dark. Cast members scream! even shriek!)

(Perhaps ten seconds pass, and the lights come back on. The stage is empty. Ten seconds pass, and **GRACE** *peaks out from the center of the curtain. She emerges, enters to show her wedding dress is covered with a white robe.)*

GRACE. Thank you all for your support. I cannot believe, even now, that it all happened. But in the one year that has since elapsed, I have heard everything turned out well.

(In full nun's habit, **ELEANOR** *enters, passes* **GRACE** *as if she does not see her, exits.)*

Instead of commitment to a sanitarium, Eleanor was allowed to enter a convent for religious instruction. There she has as many sisters as one could ask for.

*(***MR. & MRS. NEVILLE** *enter with* **JOHN**, *walk across the stage, exits.)*

Father retired. And John married a nurse. She now takes care of mother's diet, prodding, and fistula.

*(***BETH** *crosses with* **COLONEL HUNTINGTON**, *enters, then exits.)*

And the biggest shock of all. It seems that when all was said and done, Beth was more superficial than I supposed. A new dress every month and a large house were enough to secure her company – for a few years, anyway.

(**HENRY** *enters, crosses alone, exits.*)

Henry left his father's businesses and concentrated his efforts on raising his horses. He never married, worshipping my memory for the rest of his life.

(beat)

As for me, I and my nerves are at peace. Peace from jealousy, scheming, deceit, pettiness…Truthfully, I have never been so happy.

NAOMI. *(offstage)* Grace? Grace is that you?

(*Wearing a white robe,* **NAOMI** *enters from behind, stands next to* **GRACE** *whose face remains frozen in a cold stare.*)

It is you. I cannot believe it. How long have you been here?

GRACE. One year.

NAOMI. One year? And we have not come across one another sooner? It is hard to believe.

(**NAOMI** *giggles.*)

That is a fine robe. Is it linen? It is linen, is it not? I know a woman who does very fine bead work. She can do anything, hats, bags…anything!

GRACE. Good.

NAOMI. And speaking of hats – I have learned to sew artificial flowers so they make such delightful designs – roses, and irises, and lilies, and…and…

(*Still in horror,* **GRACE** *nods.*)

I am sure there are other flowers. I cannot think of them just now.

(*She giggles, swings an arm around the now shuddering* **GRACE**, *leads her to the right.*)

Oh, I am so happy we are together. What fun we shall have!

(**NAOMI** *cackles loudly. The two exit right.*)

End of Play

Also by
LEON KAYE...

**GUESS WHO'S COMING
TO SEDER**

WHERE THERE'S NO WILL

www.ingramcontent.com/pod-product-compliance
Lightning Source LLC
Chambersburg PA
CBHW070641120726
47909CB00004B/1537